Sackett's brook, which flows through Putney village and across the upper end of the Kathan meadows, was evidently so named by John Kathan, at the time of his settlement in 1752, from... a resolute chief named Sackett.

History of Captain John Kathan:
The First Settler of Dummerston, Vermont
by David L. Mansfield, 1902.

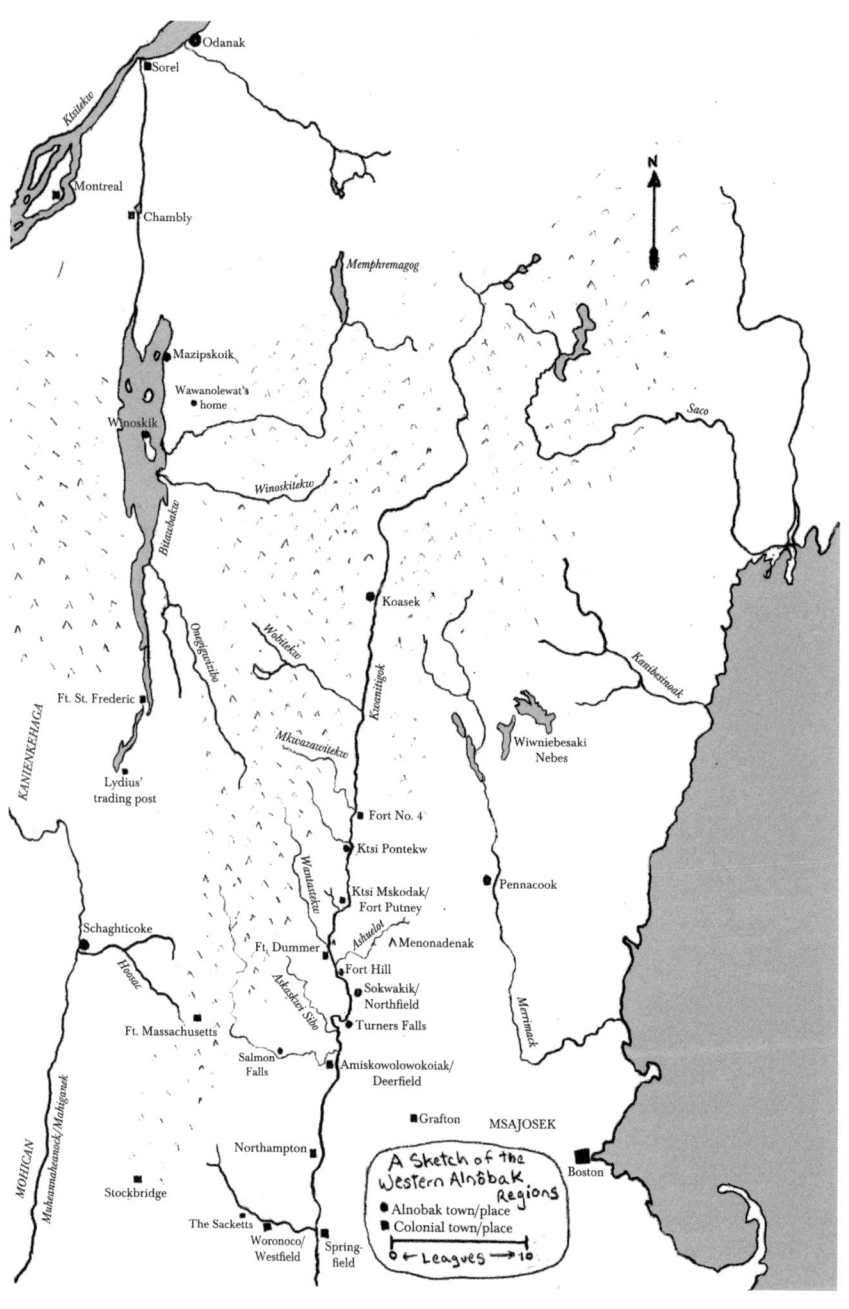

1682

Morning dawned in the east, ragged and bleak. The family didn't say much, moving about the frame house like slaves beneath a harsh taskmaster. The inner voice said, *Work hard, out of necessity. Chop and stack wood. Try not to think about the night before.*

John spent early spring clearing land, and along with the family he'd sawn and skidded two of the five acres of clearcut he needed to keep the frontier grant he'd exchanged with Deacon Chapin, who invested in the governor's program to push boundaries west. Better land than the lot he'd had—further from town, but less boggy, plenty of logs. Wood crowded the house in large piles on three sides: split wedges for firewood, fence posts, lumber, recently hauled logs waiting for attention, scraggly branches reaching to grab hold of roots or get under other logs as if to resist burning and destruction. Neatly adzed, caulked logs made the walls of the house—conifer, mostly, the medium-sized pine and hemlock from where his cornfield now rose from the rich, sloping earth of the Westfield river basin. A few other people found hollows of cleared, arable land, but he started mostly with forest. Oxen ripped out the roots of most trees; larger ones, he burned out. Plowing was harder than anything he'd ever done before, and he bordered the fields with new soapstone walls—beautiful blue, red, grey, smooth and slippery in the rain.

And fighting Indians—well, he'd come a long way from being the first white child in Newtown in 1632. His father's friend Roger Williams accompanied the Sacketts aboard the *Lyon* en route to America before Williams' banishment west to Rhode Island territory. John's grandfather Bloomfield took part in the

Pequot massacre, though he was too small to remember. When John first moved to Woronoco, as it were then called, he'd traded freely with the local natives. For a little liquor, he could get bear-skin, deer pelts, knives, and valuable knowledge of the land.

Thing was, he got in trouble with the colonial power players. The Pynchons held a virtual monopoly on trade with the Indians, and required exclusive barter and sales at their truck-houses, of which the closest were in Springfield. They were able to manipulate the small town, Pilgrim inclinations to fear trade with the savages, especially in alcohol, and to make it generally illegal. John was hauled into Pynchon's court, early on, but had the fines remitted because they could not prove the barter had occurred. Since then he had to deny any trading opportunities, which the Algonquins clearly resented. His personal relations with them grew menacing. They didn't like people who traded with them one day, then suddenly dried up permanently. They resented the Pynchon monopoly.

Since then, out on the frontier, the threat of violence loomed constantly. Sackett fought in some skirmishes, and though he knew over fifty Indians personally, most weren't nice to him. They stayed aloof, eyeing each other warily at close quarters. Always a delicate relationship.

He ran across Indians at the edge of his property ten or twelve times during this past summer; native families frequently passed through town headed north and west, from the eastern part of the colony, which soldiers had nearly purged of the strange, savage people.

At this point, like the rest of the villagers, Sackett considered these refugees as curious social oddities, like misguided children, or an unusual breed of waterfowl. If only they weren't so deadly. The deadliness sharpened his family's wits some—put an edge on the basic, everyday experience of life.

The Indian raids had resurged, now, following a quiet spell—a serious war raged a number of years earlier, with brutal attacks at Hadley, Deerfield, and Longhill, southwest of Springfield; settlers retaliated at Northfield, and natives treated them to crop and livestock destruction at Hatfield; a big wave of people came through one time, and Major Talcot gave chase and captured twenty of them right nearby, on the west bank of the Housatonic, and killed another hundred at least; the few remaining Indians throughout the Massachusetts colony bitterly resented the colonists, saying they spread disease, and withheld powder and shot. This hatred solidified into outright hostility in 1674, when a huge uprising of southern New England Indians formed under the chief the Wampanoag called Metacom, and the English called King Philip—during that conflict, they burned Sackett's own barn to the ground—in October—and killed his livestock. Jim Cornish suffered too, and Ambrose Fowler lost all his buildings. Major Treat moved a garrison to Westfield a few weeks before, but the men were called to Springfield, arriving just in time to watch it burn from across the river. The citizens were ordered to Springfield for safety, but many refused to go. All in all, it became a hectic and frightening period.

Five years ago, the massacre down at Captain Turner's falls put a grisly end to that phase of war. It was said they burned or shot three hundred Indians in their wigwams, early in the morning as they woke—older men, women, children. 'Easy prey but hell to pay,' the saying went among the colonists. Not long after, the war ended—King Philip killed, his head put on a stake—and the eastern Indians capitulated. But out on the western side of the colony the frontier was anything but safe, and it was wise to keep one ear open even while sleeping.

For years, to the north and east, bands of pillaging Pocumtuck, Abenaki and Frenchmen wreaked havoc. In the late '70s they took a lot of punishment along the rivers, with that notable rout down in Sheffield by Major Talcot's hardened soldiers. The local savages mostly pushed northwest, now spread thin throughout the woods, reaching to the northern Hudson, and all the way to their French allies in Canada.

Some were bloodthirsty villains. In the Westfield area, a young Woronoke sachem called Greylock had a sly way of persecuting, or punishing locals—sometimes merely pulling latch strings to open doors at night, letting livestock loose, or letting in the cold—and other times visiting destruction upon them, killing cattle, sheep, or pigs, burning individual houses, barns, dry fields—now and then, killing and scalping or abducting the settlers. Few had actually seen him—and those who did were often wives he singled out, to terrorize. Their traumatized descriptions of him grew increasingly monstrous in the telling and retelling, and terror hung thick in the air, especially after dark.

The memory of 1675 flooded back on Sackett now—the sound of crackling while he loaded the musket; through gaps in the wall the Sacketts saw lights dancing in the treetops. They knew it was the barn, with its large store of hay in the loft catching as only dry grass can.

Back in '75 the greenhorn frontier family would have liked to cower from native raiders, but after so much labor, they had to fight. He and Junior loaded and cocked the muskets quickly, and holding his knife in one hand and the musket in the other, John kicked up the latch and burst into the yard. He saw three or four figures running near the barn, and they began to whoop as they saw him. He ran toward them and fired at the closest, then grabbed a firebrand and chased one, though not into the woods. Bill stood close behind him, only twelve, carrying a shovel; Junior fired his musket, and knelt to reload. Back then, Abigail needed to fight as well.

"John, take this! I'll load your gun." Abigail held out a loaded pistol, which he took, and she grabbed the Brown Bess, looking wildly around, then setting quickly to work with the powder and ramrod.

"Thanks, Abby. Now get back! Get inside! Can you blow the horn?" A minute later the horn sounded in the hollow, and help arrived after five terrifying minutes. Fowlers and Grangers came from down the road, and Deweys from up the road—four men and seven teenage boys, all armed.

"How is it, John? How many?" And soon they'd chased out the attackers, pitched in to control the fire, and began scouting field perimeters along properties up and down Sackett's Ridge.

The barn crumbled in a smouldering heap before they all gave in for the night, with only a few base logs salvageable after the last leaping flames were quenched. Exhausted, John and Abigail gathered the animals and tied them to posts. The next morning John began to rebuild, starting with a simple shelter and paddock, and—ambitious man that he was—a new dam for a sawmill.

They were seven long years since. Other than a big feud with the Deweys over the millpond, things seemed quiet. But now, in 1682, predators stalked the edge of his little clearing again.

This time, the savages had struck a weighty blow. Nine hours before, still awake in bed, John heard low, throaty calls, like a group of barred owls passing through. He knew better. He roused his wife Abigail, pulled the string inside to seal the door latch, and checked the heavy wooden shutters. The bigger children slept in the loft, but downstairs Elizabeth lay wide awake, her eyes following her parents' movements about the twenty-foot square cabin, listening to their worried whispers. A clear night beckoned outside, lit by a quarter moon, and tree silhouettes surrounded the two large clearings—the house, barn, and paddock nested in the smaller, and in the other, pasture and vegetable garden, with corn to the hips—not wheat but native American maize, and big-leafed squash plants sprawling in a generous patch. John pulled a loaded Brown Bess off the gun rack over the door, and peered through a chink in the heavy wooden wall into the better-lit part of the yard. Dark, human shapes flitted through the night. He climbed the ladder and shook his sons awake.

"Get your gun, Johnny. We got visitors. Hey Bill, get up! Indians." He jumped down, took up the dry powder horn, and quickly, carefully sprinkled a charge into the flintlock.

"Bill, you take this pistol. Take the cutlass." He held out the weapons. "Careful where you point that. It's liable to go off. When you see your target, aim small, you'll miss small. Center of the body. Let's get outside." They threw open the door and peered into the shadowy dooryard beyond.

Sackett stepped out the front door, followed by his sons.

Wasting no time, he and the boys ran out and circled the barn, well armed. Abigail ran seventy yards from the cabin to bring another loaded gun, finding them quietly pointing toward the black edge of the field, where the woods began. "Did you see movement there, Abby?"

"No, John. I can't see a thing."

"Mum! Dad!" The screams came from the house. Turning, the Sacketts sprinted back to the cabin to check on the girls, who stood by the door—Mary, Abby, and Hannah. Mary held a pitchfork. Where was Elizabeth? Her small bed lay empty, and a few frantic seconds of peering around the cabin led to panic, and Hannah confirmed their fears.

"They took Elizabeth!" The teenager stared at her parents in horror; her voice choked, her body shaking violently.

Abigail yelled, "No!" She ran toward the wood with John after her. He caught her at the edge.

"Abby, let us! I'll get Maynard Granger and the boys, and go after her. Johnny and Bill, guard the house, and kill 'em if you can! The bastards stole your sister!"

John Sackett ran off down the road, and presently brought six men who raced into the woods with torches and guns, tearing along the path, circling off into the woods wherever there was an opening. They found, saw, and heard nothing. After about a mile, they listened carefully to the riotous katydids, crickets, and cicadas.

"John, I don't know. I don't hear a thing."

"They could be gone in any direction."

"Not much hope, I think, John."

"Just stand still for a minute. Quiet." John wasn't ready to give up. They all listened for over five minutes. Then they started circling back.

John's shoulders sagged, and Abigail gasped a pair of quiet sobs as they reentered the house.

Morning dawned in the east, ragged and bleak. And again.

Abigail lay awake through two quiet, moonlit nights, staring up into the dark roof of the cabin, teary at times, imagining the experiences of her six-year-old daughter. The children twisted in their beds, beset by troubled dreams, off and on for weeks.

For her part, Elizabeth stared at the sky, traumatized. Her head hurt, jolted until she finally fell asleep, carried many hours like a potato sack after the horrible man snatched her from her house. She'd tried to hide under her small bed as she saw him look at his sisters; then he came toward her, and her effort proved futile. The dark, powerful man lifted her in the cabin and carried her quickly into the dark forest while she screamed and beat his back. She fought as hard as she could.

She bounced rhythmically, inexorably, on the man's shoulder. The man ran smooth, fast, and didn't seem to mind the weight. She couldn't imagine how far she'd traveled—further than she'd ever been in that amount of time. Eventually, she'd been shaken senseless, exhausted, with a mounting fear that she'd lost her family forever.

A dream began—she lay on her bedstead, in the dark, alone. She heard scratching outside, on the walls, and muffled voices she couldn't understand. Then a thump, and the door opened to reveal a black shape, a shadow that reached out and grabbed her, pulling her away. She fought, screamed, but she couldn't shake it off—the vice-like arms pulled her out the cabin.

She woke with a terrified start against a mossy bank. The strange men sat around a fire, mostly awake—three seemed asleep, or at least resting. They were six in all. She looked around, eyes wide with fear.

At home the Sacketts wore cloth, linen under wool, with leather shoes, but these men wore nothing but leather. They had thin, well-tied moccasins and breechcloths, they had belts and straps and pouches, and some had longbows with a thin birch-bark quiver—two had muskets. In addition to her abject horror at what might happen next, she felt uncomfortable near their naked torsos.

One saw she lay awake, and shook the others. They rose to their feet. One of the men had long, dark hair with a grey lock in the middle of his forehead, and he handed the girl some cooked fish on a large leaf. "*Wicinek*," he said. "Eat." She ate it, being careful not to swallow the bones. They spoke to her again: "You walk fast." This came not as a comment, but a command.

They set off at a difficult pace for the six-year-old, pushing her from behind if she tried to slow down. Soon she realized she could run very slowly, stay with them, and not get overly tired. After a while, they reached a stream. They indicated she should drink, and she did. The pool reflected green leaves and the trunks of black birch and hemlock; smooth, black rocks showed beneath the surface of the water. She drank deeply, very thirsty.

They ran off and on all day, with alternate breaks, and most of the time someone carried the little girl, which was much easier for her.

They passed through deep wooded vales, tamarack bogs, hardwood uplands, over increasingly large hills, until she became sore and exhausted. She was given some sort of nut cake and a mixture of black and red, a tart, chewy dried fruit—seedy, but very tasty. Clean water abounded. No one had done anything bad to her, besides running her ragged. She'd been too scared to try and resist today; even at her young age, she'd heard of gauntlets, scalping, starvation and other bad situations captured people ran into. After dark, she passed out on dry grass at the edge of their small encampment, worn beyond anything she'd known before. She didn't dream that night. She woke comfortable, though aching, in the morning. The men all lay around for about two hours, enjoying the warm sun and the singing birds. Elizabeth didn't mind a slow start after yesterday's ordeal.

A small, mossy stream lay close at hand, and she leaned over, splashed her face, and watched some crayfish shooting around backwards. Loss and fear palpably stabbed her heart after five minutes or so. She dealt with the fear, the loss, as best she could. The Indians gave her space, trying not to approach her more than necessary. Eventually they got back on the trail, with a more leisurely pace.

At the end of the second full day, having crossed into a series of low mountains, they came to a hole in the side of the largest mountain she had ever seen. Inside, a nice floor of flat earth gave ample room for six people to rest, cook, and sleep. Many hidden supplies lay tucked away, including cooking equipment: a sheet of metal and a rounded clay pot with a fluted edge. The men grilled birds, vegetables and especially nuts, which they had in large supply. They slept late again the following morning.

She had of course observed the men very carefully, in mortal fear they would take some sudden action against her. She tried to read their faces, which seemed impossible. Eventually she began to find them fascinating. She noted that in addition to bows, (one had a pistol holstered in soft leather) they carried only a

Praise for Sackett

Stuart Strothman has written an engaging and balanced re-telling of the 18th century wars which created New England and America out of ancient indigenous peoples' homelands. It in-cludes not only the horror of the warfare and enmity between the English/Yankee newcomers and the Abenaki, Sokwaki, Pocumtuc, Mohican, and Kanienkehaga (Mohawk); this vital novel explores the kinship and depth of enduring connections between the Native and non-Native peoples which is the true leg-acy of that time period. From familiar geographic place names derived from the Abenaki and other indigenous languages to the many traditions and gifts of living which have become a central part of rural, northeastern life, this work illuminates the shared landscape, familial and historical relations, and hidden histo-ries of cooperation which still provide the cultural backbone of American society.

John Moody
Ethnohistorian of the Winter Center for Indigenous Traditions

Stuart Strothman's novel accurately describes the eighteenth-century frontier of New England and New York and one family's existence despite having a foot in two worlds—Native and Anglo-American. With a keen eye and cultural sensitivity, Strothman effectively treats this family over several generations. Besides careful descriptions of Alnobak/Abenaki culture, colonial his-tory, and the Northeast's landscape, the author shows the pres-sures this family faced. He sympathetically describes the Native peoples' struggles to survive in a rapidly changing world, being caught in the middle of colonial rivalries as well as longstanding conflicts with their Native American enemies.

Laurence M. Hauptman
SUNY Distinguished Professor Emeritus of History

Using research and imagination, Stuart Strothman adds an Abenaki story to the historical fiction of New England—a genre in which Native people rarely appear as believable characters—and shows that in the Connecticut Valley as in many other regions of early America, Indian and English lives and family histories intertwined.

Colin Calloway
Dartmouth Professor of History and Native American Studies

In his novel, Stuart Strothman uses the abduction of Elizabeth Sacket by Native Americans about 1682 to highlight the cultural differences that caused years of conflict. She was raised by the Native Americans, accepted their way of life, and married one of the tribe. One can only imagine how differently things would have been if, instead of war, the Natives and the Colonists had been able to have come to an agreement on their differences.

Thurmon King
Sackett Historian for The Sackett Family Association

Sackett

by Stuart Strothman

Set in Baskerville.
This font was created in 1757
by John Baskerville
of Birmingham, England.

Self-published by the author with the assistance of
Pumpelly Press, a division of Surry Cottage Books
800 Park Avenue, Suite 111A
Keene, New Hampshire 03431

Second Edition

ISBN: 978-0-9829853-9-7

few simple things in small pouches, with which they could do an amazing number of tasks. Each had a knife of some sort in a sheath around the neck; though most were metal, one was stone. One had a braided coil of rope apparently made from coarse, rubbed bark, which he set down at camp. She rubbed a bight between her fingers, and it felt surprisingly smooth.

They cut saplings, whittled tools, mended leather; they shot pigeons, and one snared a partridge one morning (she could tell by his description to the others, when he came back with the bird); they caught fish with hooks, quickly woven baskets, and sometimes with their hands, tickling their undersides and flipping them out of the water, or running them into narrow spaces; they climbed trees, and gathered and munched plants she'd never seen before; they talked at length, and pointed at things with their chins. They swam beautifully, and ran tirelessly, their feet stepping one in front of the other on narrow paths. They didn't seem to know English, but were adept at quick, nonverbal instructions. They had long, black hair in ponytails tied in two or three places.

Two of them tended to smile at the little girl, and seemed friendly. Another, more serious, had shown her how to sharpen and tie a wooden hook one afternoon at the edge of a mountain lake, and tried to teach her some words in his language. He seemed like he might be twenty, but he was strong, and regarded her sternly—he was tall, and he carried more equipment than the others (which still wasn't much, she thought). His face showed deep pockmarks, and he had two long scars across his left arm.

The man with the grey widow's peak seemed young as well, barely older than the scarred man. He seemed to be the one they looked to for direction, which he gave in a steady and succinct manner. The scarred man also carried weight, and when there was a discussion they all voiced their opinions, which the girl could not understand. Decisions seemed to be unanimous.

They spoke only rarely. She could tell they tried to be friendly, in their way; they gave her the best bits of food, and tried to make her comfortable. They managed this reasonably well, considering that she no longer had a roof over her head at night, and the safety of four thick wooden walls. Dry moss felt softer than the lumpy, rope-supported mattress she and her little sister had shared, and besides, she dropped to the ground exhausted every night. By the time they reached the lake, her muscles were hardening, and she felt fast and strong like never before. Her legs were sore! Layers of soreness.

That afternoon brought another hard hike—she was often carried—and in the night it rained. They lay under a thick cover of leafy branches the men constructed while the ground was still dry. Late in the overcast afternoon of the third day, they came into a settlement at the edge of a large, healthy river.

She entered the village in file with the six men, with four of them in front. An array of people regarded them as they arrived, and a man came up to them.

"Hi you, girl. You okay? These men nice, won't hurt you. You been away from your family days now, yes? Don't worry, now. It's hard you being away from home, but we take care of you. Find you home...good people. At least for now. Don't worry." The man with the grey lock scowled at this intruder, chastised him in a different language, and then motioned toward two dome-shaped, bark houses and a long half-cylinder house with a curved roof that looked like it held many people. They walked across the well-worn dirt road, and into the larger building.

Three women puttered inside, and three evenly spaced campfires marked the centers of three separate rooms separated by flaps in a small but long, low house with a curved roof, which looked like a huge cylinder set partway in the ground. The fires sent up smoke from pits in the floor. Three holes gaped in the roof, wide open for smoke to escape. The oldest of the women tended the central fire, and soon the young girl decided this was the young grey-haired man's home, and this woman, his partner. She didn't know if these people married, as her parents had before she was born. The man moved around the home in comfort, looking over weapons, scooping a bowl of soup from the clay tureen, sitting on his heels near the fire.

The man gestured toward a place for Elizabeth to make herself comfortable, in a low, bunk-like platform set off to the side of the room. She climbed in and rested on a thin straw mat covered with fur, which she felt certain was deerskin. It smelled rich and smoky, and not unpleasant. She was overcome by a sense of exhaustion; this arrival seemed to herald the end of her stressful travel, and with possible time ahead to reflect on her separation from her parents, she immediately fell asleep, her head thick, her body achy and stuffed with cotton, her thoughts fuzzy.

When she woke, she still felt leaden and achy. Evening had begun to set in. The space seemed low, dark and hazy, and the women worked together, making different kinds of food, including a maize porridge, roasted birds and fresh greens. The smells enticed her, though the smoke hurt her eyes a bit. She lay, quietly watching, like a forest animal.

The women spoke to her at times—"*gagiwidahozo*" and "*wijihlamid*" and other unintelligible commentary, accompanied by gestures and smiles. They tried speaking what she thought was probably French, but she understood none of it. She worried they were pagan, or possibly Catholic, which according to her father ranked as bad or worse. But the women seemed kind; they gave her a bowl of water, made from a gourd, and tried to accommodate her needs without bothering her too much. One of them showed her where to relieve herself, and how to wash up. When they offered her a bowl of porridge (called *sagamitay*), she took it. They didn't speak any English, at least to her.

She ate, and soon two more men came in and ate as well (making seven people in this house, with maybe a quarter the floorspace of her little cabin in Westfield, and only half as tall—Elizabeth stayed fixed in her bunk, which seemed the only available place for her). They talked a little with the women, but mostly among themselves. The strange language rambled softly along like a babbling brook, or the path of a butterfly. The men lay about, smoking, while the women worked away at what seemed like a hundred things. The long, arched indoors—with three fires and no chimney—were often filled with woodsmoke, and breathing came harder here than at home. It looked surreal to her, this flickering world of reddish bodies, strange language, strange scenery, with her mind thick and foggy. It seemed another world, far removed from her home. She fell asleep again, and after a few hours dreamt strange dreams of traveling over mountains, and playing with fire. The dreams felt vivid and real, and waking life hazy and unreal, and she woke and slept and could not tell the difference, tossing through the night. She carried a ball of tension in her lower back for days, passing in and out of delirious sleep, unable or unwilling to get out of bed.

Finally, she awoke, and felt she could not lie in that bed any longer. She rose. She came to the edge of the fire, centrally located in the bark hut. A pot hung there, with hot corn mash and a ladle, and clean wooden bowls nearby. She took some food, and ate with her fingers, as she had seen others do. The woman in charge (this seemed to be her house) came in and smiled, and embraced the little girl. She offered her a damp cloth and a large bowl of warm water, and a primitive cake of soap, which might have been ash and bear tallow, to wash up. She hung a flap of deerskin to give her some privacy. Elizabeth understood, and took her time, washing away some of her old self as she took in the smells of the household. They were rich and inviting. The woman gave her a clean set of clothes, in the Indian style—a dipping collar, loose fitting around the waist and wrist. The cloth was strong, but softer than the wool she was used to wearing. There was a leather skirt and moccasins. She put them on, feeling clean and otherworldly. She remained silent, and began to explore her surroundings.

In the following days, Elizabeth had freedom to look around the house, and the tiny village. She quietly wandered, observing racks of drying fish, drying herbs, drying corn, hanging blankets and clothing, and many different kinds of houses, all rounded in some way. The wind blew across her face. The houses moved air well, but remained perfectly dry even in a driving rain. She remembered her stuffy, damp, rectangular frame house in Westfield, and did not miss it.

There were many different people too, clearly not all from the same groups. Some men wore ponytails, and the rest of their head shaven; others had close-cropped hair, especially on the side they used to draw a bow; still others grew it long, like the men she had arrived with, wearing a thick ponytail tied in several places. Many had extensive tattooing. They seemed able to talk easily together, joked quite a bit, and generally got along very well. Many people were tall, much taller than adults she had known in Westfield. Some seemed sad, broken in spirit, their eyes staring at unfixed points, seeming not to notice Elizabeth as she walked by.

Younger boys were given to quite a bit of roughhousing. They didn't seem to work much at all. Though they stared sometimes, they didn't otherwise bother her as she watched them shove, and sometimes wrestle one another. They seemed happy, healthy, proud, and very loud compared with the mostly silent adults. Sometimes the teenagers played games of daring, balancing high on tree limbs, playing catch with knives, or holding coals to their arms, showing no reaction at all. No one stopped any of this play, and, even stranger, nobody ever seemed angry with any of the children.

The women had more similar dress, though there were a few noticeable differences in the style of clothing. Women and girls, in general, remained in motion, tending fields, harvesting, drying, and grinding corn; they braided the shocks for mats, shucked and stored ears in large, bark-covered baskets, made clothing, repaired houses.

A few dogs roamed around, and large wooden boats and a wide variety of smaller canoes lay along the shore. There were eight or ten children of different ages who ran in the roads, playing games, looking at her, talking, and smiling. One small boy a few years older than her followed her around at a distance, seeming inquisitive. A couple of men who seemed to be passing through from the opposite side of town spoke to her, once, in limited English:

"You girl, you came from Massachusetts? Woronoco? What you call Westfield? Don't you worry to be here, these are good people. This land here, we all meet in. European people kill us off, push us out. We gather here and elsewhere. Now you with the Woronoke. They take care of you."

She summoned the courage to ask, "where are you from?" They pointed east, and said, "We are Mohican, from Mahiganek." But that didn't mean anything to her. And in general, everyone spoke another language, and avoided English.

She eventually gave up, preferring not to speak at all. It suited her; she wasn't ready to talk, she decided. Much of the day, and in the evening, she lay quietly in her little bed and watched the three families in her house, occasionally talking, laughing, or speaking sharply to one another. The personalities were very different, and she started to learn a few words, just by watching and listening. Nobody frightened her. They offered her food and showed her where to get water.

Three weeks after she arrived, a new relative whom she hadn't met, a mature, friendly woman, came into the house and the families greeted her with hugs and a lot of incomprehensible jabber. Soon they all began to look at the girl, and she knew they were talking about her. Then the woman spoke to her.

"Girl, your hair is beautiful. My name is Mejejaawi. We've been calling you Golden Hair. In our language, that is *wizwame odembkwan*. We just call you Wizwame. What do you think of this place so far? These women are kind women, I have known them for years. You don't need to be afraid here. I know it's different."

Elizabeth finally responded, speaking slowly. "You speak well. You know English?"

"I lived many years with an English woodsman, who didn't care much for your towns, and preferred to be on his own. He was pilloried—that's what you call it? Which they made him stand on a stage in the middle of town where people looked at him and yelled things, or threw things at him. He was accused of stealing, but he didn't do it, and the real problem was he didn't go to church enough, or so he said. Anyway he went west and trapped in the woods near Sheffield years back, and we came to know each other when I was a teenager at Stockbridge. We fell in love, and then we stayed away from the whites, who treated us worse than dirt. He taught me English, and I worked on his Algonkian. He's just dead now, just a few weeks ago. I have traveled a short way to join your family. These people here, and me, we all used to live where we took you from, before you did."

"My father told me no one lived there."

"Well, that isn't true. We called that spot where your cabin is Tomhaumaucke, because water came down the sides of the hill evenly. When your people started to come in. We were killed and pushed out, mostly because so many of us died from potent diseases—scarlet fever, smallpox, typhoid. We were thin and broken just eight years ago, and one morning soldiers came into our village and burned what was left of it. They let us run, north and west. We spent time briefly at Stockbridge with a lot of others—Mohican, Pocumtuck, Sokwaki. It was a sad place there, so many people torn from their land, their homes, with many relatives passing on in recent memory. The British who ran the town were strict, and we hated them. The eyes of people in that place seemed lost, hopeless, and everyone was just passing through. Some got sick, some packed and headed west, some got organized. Governor Andros planted a tree in Schaghticoke, which you can see in the middle of the village. He called it the Tree of Welfare, and invited our *sôgemô* Soquans and all of our people to come live under its spreading branches. This family came north a few years ago, here, to make a home while we can still be together. Since then, many of our old families have split off and headed west, to the mountains of Mahiganek. Others go north, to Mazipskoik on Bitawbákw, the lake between Hodinohso:ni and the Wôbanakiak."

The woman looked the girl in the eye. "Your people—the British, especially—are always pushing, scowling. They hate us, they kill us. They think land can be owned, and bought with money, and they can make it so with their power. Which we think they are mostly evil, and we have lost so many people, so we take them when we can. Young people, like you." She said suddenly, "What do you think of this place?"

"I don't know...I miss my family." Tears came to her eyes as she spoke, and the women all saw her pain and sadness. Mejejaawi put her hand on the girl's shoulder.

"We don't want you hurt. But we need you here."

"Tell me about these people. Who are they? I met two men today who spoke to me—they were dressed differently. Where are all these people from?" They were mature questions for such a young girl, but she was mature, observant, she'd been watching quietly for over two weeks, and she wanted to know.

"They are mostly Pocumtuck clans—what is left from the areas where you live—Springfield, Westfield, Deerfield, Northhampton.

We are Woronoke, but some are Agawam, Nonatick or Sokwakiak, from up the river Connecticut, which we call the Kwanitekw. Wôbanakiak call themselves Alnôbak, the 'regular people.' There are many Mohicans here too, and assorted others, in a nearby village. Mohicans are from Muheannaheanock, the big river that flows both north and south, which lies to the west. Some call them River Indians. This old man here"—and she pointed and laughed at the grey-haired young man who stole Elizabeth from her family, and whose house she now sat in. He watched them calmly as they spoke, and his eyes widened a bit in good humor—"is my younger brother, Wawanolewat—the name means he fools others, easy! He misses our home soil sure enough, which was where you lived, same as him when he was a child, in Woronoco—we called that little part Tomhaumucke, as I said. Our family stayed there for part of every year. That is the place we like most to visit, when raiding colonists. A few years back we burned a barn on that site." Elizabeth could not remember that, but she had certainly heard of it.

"Wawanolewat is a powerful—you understand? He's our clan leader now, and a war sachem as well. He's a good man, with a powerful spirit. Our brother is Malalemet, and the two of them are close; they hunt together, go to war together whenever possible. His home fire is that one, there." She indicated the third firepit in the long, half-cylinder, bark house. "You will remember him—the tall one with the scars on the arm. He was with Wawanolewat when they took you. But he has headed north, to Mazipskoiodanak, to parley with Wôbanakiak elders and the French."

"Your brothers seem good to you, but they burned my barn. They stole me." Elizabeth felt scared, making this accusation, and her eyes began to water with grief.

Shaking her head, but looking at her compassionately, the woman said, "Colonists take our land. They kill us. They are fools, who do not know the land. Yes, we burn their barns. We didn't know your family." She seemed to think that explanation should justify things.

The girl didn't speak for minute or so.

"These women...may I please know, what are their names?" Elizabeth appeared old, showing both her curiosity and her manners.

"Atahla, there. This is her house, really." She indicated the woman by the central fire, who kept working and did not look up. "She is with Wawanolewat, these five years and more. That woman is Ntôna, over there." She indicated a teenager with a wide face, who smiled at the girl. She had a gap between her two front teeth, and thick, dark hair, well combed. "She is wife to Malalemet."

"This is Oladaka." She grasped the third woman's hand and touched her shoulder as she said this, as the beautiful young woman was seated right next to her. The woman looked up, and Elizabeth took in her eyes, kind and careworn, her smile. "Another sister to myself and the brothers. We are lucky to have four children from our family left alive. Her husband is Jajigwiwi, which you've seen many times.

Mejejaawi smiled. "I have had five children. Three are gone. Two are alive. I have one son, one daughter. My son is already old enough to hunt and fight—he's off in the dawnland, the woods to the northeast, south of Canada. My daughter now lives in this village, too. You will meet her soon. Her husband is killed. She has a boy, only four years old. These children are all your brothers and sisters now. We will all live with you now, in this house."

Elizabeth took this in. "Why didn't you come sooner? So I could talk to you?"

"It is tradition for the family to wait for seven days at least before talking to the people we bring to our village. Wawanolewat speaks more than a little English." That seemed amazing to the girl; he could have spoken to her, but didn't. She wasn't sure how to feel about that.

"Where are we? This isn't Massachusetts?"

"No, we are beyond the spreading English border. We're north and east of Fort Massachusetts—you've heard of that? It's called Schaghticoke. There are more Dutch than Bostonians in this area, but right where we are, it's just us regular people. Dutch claimed this land until twenty years ago, but now the English are in control, and they'd like us to stay in a group and fight for them when they want. The Hodinohso:ni fight for them already, but we don't have the stomach to join the Bostonians. Just north and west of here is still Wôbanaki, what we call the 'dawnland.' We stay connected to our peoples, and fight. For a time, Metacom and Anawon, with many of our men, fought for the Indians, but they were beaten. The Wôbanakiak have always stood strong, Now, again, many river men have gone to fight these English colonists. Joining with Wôbanaki, striking the western settlements. My son went. But we hear it dasn't go well, and we worry for them."

The girl studied her sad, lined face, and for the first time, considered the woman's losses, and what she had been saying. Mejejaawi went down the row to her new bunk after dinner, having translated some introductions and conversation, which was very helpful after all that time. Mejejaawi explained, though, that English was generally forbidden, and this would be the last time they could speak in the girl's native tongue. They avoided the topic of her home and her parents, and talked about themselves, their relationships, and things they liked about Wizwame (that is what everyone called her). No one asked what her name had been before, and she did not mention it. When she went to bed that night, she believed she would never speak English again.

Weeks went by, and Wizwame worked hard on her new family's language. They helped her. Living things were different from dead things, and they had their own pronouns and plurals, like men and women in English. Trees and plants counted as living things, until they were cut down, and so did some other important things they valued highly, like moccasins and tobacco.

Mejejaawi's daughter Alita turned out to be a friendly young woman, and her son Abasani was a quiet, shy child who quickly developed a real fondness for his 'sister" Wizwame. Around the house, the two of them helped with bringing water, crushing corn, folding blankets—but they also played a great deal, especially with dolls that Alita taught them to weave from cornhusks, or thick grasses. Wizwame loved to make cradleboards and clothing, and act out scenes with and for Abasani, who was generally delighted with the outcomes, happy to follow her lead, happy to be playing. The two of them enjoyed many afternoons in this way. Over time, Abasani began to change the games, to make them more warlike. By this time, Wizwame liked these games too. She learned bowhunting and how to butcher animals, in addition to cooking, sewing, beading, and leather work. She learned to make baskets with a variety of materials. She learned to make overnight shelters, and to improve more permanent ones.

Midsummer sun seared her skin, but she learned to cover up with a wraparound cloth. She actually preferred to stay in the sun, because that way she avoided the *begwesak* (mosquitoes), and at night, she learned to keep a blanket nearby, or to be near the fire. The insects bothered her more than the other children, which she found intensely frustrating. Atahla finally (a day later) taught her to rub cedar bark on herself, and keep some with her, to help keep them away. Mejejaawi also spent a good deal of time translating Alnôbak and Mohican (mostly for other people who wanted to introduce themselves), and teaching her Pocumtuck languages. The girl picked up some simple Dutch as well, just for use with traders. At home, they spoke Woronoke.

She began to play with other children in the large river, called Hoosac. They taught her many names of things—rocks, cray-fish, trout, shad. They made her pictures of large, striped fish with pointed fins, painted in charcoal on white birch bark. A variety of birds flew across the water; swallows she knew, and bluebirds and finches, and the passenger pigeons in droves; but there were birds with yellow wingtips, and great blue-grey wading birds. There were large white wading birds, and smaller ones that ran in the sandy areas, and in small open fields. The hills rolled smoothly here, with an occasional grey rock outcropping to break up the hills of deciduous forest, and meadows, with thicker brush at the edges. Trees were largely hardwood—oak, maple chestnut, butternut, beech, and walnut—with majestic conifers on the hilltops. Here and there, a few birches, bronze, grey, white or paper, especially on the hillsides or the riverbanks. Some of the trees were powerful, apparently, having a god-nature that made them more closely related to people. Many animals were like this, too. People, it seemed, had a regular life and another, spiritual life, that they learned about from dreams. Some of the plants and animals were found in that world, and generally her family knew which ones they were, and taught Wizwame to respect them, and treat them like people, as much as possible.

Friendly, fun-loving children roamed freely, and had many games that they loved to play. Over the next few months, they made stone beads, chipped wood, threw stones at different targets, and skipped them in the larger pools. They played hide and seek in the woods, which was hard because they were almost silent, even in dry leaves. They could whistle marvelously with their lips and hands. Most were very daring, and all very nice, compared to children she had known in Westfield, except for one boy, Melik, who wanted to boss everyone around. He wasn't generally popular, often told summarily to close his mouth, as in the following scene:

"Abasani, let's throw rocks. You get a lot of rocks and bring them up here, and I'll hit the far tree you see right there."

"I gotta go home and help my mom."

"You have to stay. You said you would do what I wanted later."

At times like this Wizwame would chime in. "You're not the *wadebôdeb niona*, Melik—not the head of our family. If Abi needs to go, he goes. You are a small person with a big mouth, and you should keep it closed." Melik knew not to cross the daughter of Wawanolewat, and left them be.

In general, the boys seemed normal, but a little wild. They raced and wrestled. They shot arrows with metal points, and fished with bone or wood hooks and handmade string. They had one game they liked to play, where one boy would shoot arrows at another, who would dodge the flying darts. Wizwame loved to watch.

Contests among children were not the only entertainment.

Twice during the summer the village divided into two, using the river as a divider, and held contests between these "teams"— canoe tipping, wrestling, racing, lacrosse, throwing tomahawks into a log. The best advice: "Throw it like you need to kill someone, before he gets you." With the right attitude, she found it stuck nearly every time. Her family had a lot of fun rooting for people from her side of the river. None could beat Malalemet at wrestling, and Wawanolewat ranked ever among the fleetest runners.

Eventually she acquired one particular friend, the boy he saw looking curiously at her in town; he didn't seem to judge her by her differences. He was patient with her language difficulty. She had met him for the first time, walking along the river with Mejejaawi, stepping over roots. From behind a tree he suddenly appeared, and tried to wander along the edge of the path past them.

Wizwame said, "Can you ask that boy his name? He follows me." Mejejaawi said, "He is Nebilinto." He turned upon hearing his name, and they talked together. Zwame learned his family were Sokwaki, and his mother came twenty years earlier from a place called Fort Hill. Kanienkehaga, Seneca, and Onondaga lay siege to the Sokwakiak stronghold up on Fort Hill, just below the headland of Wantatstegok, and many died on both sides in a fierce battle. Their numbers were seriously reduced, because about twenty years before that, almost all the Sokwaki died of smallpox, influenza and measles.

Mejejaawi said, "They've had it as hard as anybody. Their name even means 'the people who separated.' For a long time, the land to the east and south of here was available for shared hunting—an agreement between Pocumtuck and Kanienkehaga, long honored by the Sokwakiak as well. But the latter were war-like, and they hated the English, and apparently resented the Kanienkehaga intrusion. They refused to join a carefully organized peace treaty some forty years ago, and they even killed a formal party who came to them under the flag of truce. A bad mistake, as it turned out. The Hodinohso:ni came back and killed everyone, except a few women and children who hid in food storage pits."

"Where is Wantatstegok?"

"The river mouth is north of Northfield." Northfield. The little girl remembered that name. She knew there had been sorrow there, from hearing her parents talk about it—many Indian attacks. Mejejaawi explained that just a few years ago, white people had finally driven the last Indians away from the Sokwakiak land, and destroyed their houses and cornfields. Over the sad generations the Sokwakiak migrations led many places, including a new village called Odanak, like Schaghticoke, but way up north among the Frenchmen.

Winter came, with no hope of returning to Massachusetts. As the cold began to set in, they bent back the flexible saplings which supported the house, and tucked in layers of reed mats, which insulated beautifully. Their clothing was ingenious—over her moccasins she wore a moose hock boot, and her legs and torso had four layers, mostly made with beaver pelt and bearskin. She had ermine undergarments. They had numerous cloth blankets from Dutch traders out of Beverwyck. As a result she felt warm and friendly in the long *wigwôm*, and there was plenty of food until midwinter. Later, in the dead of winter, none of them ate much, and she often didn't stir from her bed where there were plenty of furs, unless it was warm enough to run and play in the snow. They made her tightly stitched, fur-lined clothing, which she wore constantly, only removing her long moccasins when she was near the fire. The people ate a variety of dried vegetables and corn dishes, and whenever an animal was brought in, they shared out the fattiest parts and devoured solid inner organs with obvious delight. The women gave her all kinds of games and activities that she could do during her waking hours in bed, and began to teach her to sew and weave, and to cook. She liked to grind corn, called *skamonal,* with the long, smooth stone pestle on one of the flat rocks with a small, bowl-shaped mortar in the middle. So, she passed the winter.

The spring came, slowly at first, and then with a rush; the ground softened and warmth flowed back into the land. She experienced the rebirth of plants, and the feathery growth of new leaves like never before—it was a miracle, experienced every day. Her new family was good to her, kind, and endlessly interesting. She played and worked, worked and played and slept.

A miraculous run of huge, striped fish (she had seen drawings last year) came up the river, well into spring, and a celebration and feast ensued with rich, tender white steaks served with sweet sauces and fresh vegetables. Thousands of smaller, silver fish came up too, and they were fun to catch in baskets, and good to eat, though bony. Some of these silver fish were very oily, with a black spot just behind the gills. People seemed to like these best of all.

When the heady period of river play and fishing ended,

summer was again underway, and corn, beans and squash grew in small fields, a familiar sight for the little girl. She was quickly learning the language; she was strong, clean, and healthy, and surprisingly cheerful. Years went on. Little Zwame stayed with her Woronoke family. She remained good friends with Nebilinto, and they often walked in the woods together. He taught her the Alnôbak names of many important trees: *Senomozi, Wobimizi, Koasek Abasiak, Maskwamozi.* Zwame and the boy matched well in looks and wit, and early into their teenage years, they grew sweet on one another. In time, they became as one.

1703

These were dark times. The good years of her youth quickly passed into enduring violence along the Kwanitekw, and the family moved north. The king of France, Louis XIV, put his grandson on the throne in Spain, and England, the Netherlands, and the Hapsburg Empire declared war as a result. Boatloads of English soldiers headed north on the river from Deerfield and Northfield and killed when they could; the Alnôbak and Kanienkehagak allied with the French against England didn't hesitate to do the same. A group of French Canadians invited Zwame's family to move north, to a village in the woods near Fort Chambly, as there was a summary feeling that they were too much in danger at their home on the brook south of the falls, so close to English settlements. They had moved during the early spring, so they could plant and prepare for winter in their new home, and their small patch of *skamonal* grew well, in better soil along the Richelieu River. Chambly was a center of the *temakwak* economy, but the primary family trade was in baskets and healing herbs.

Little things—common knowledge among dawnlanders—fascinated the French doctors. Infusions of *kokokhoakok* would help a scrape, *sasôksekak* a rash; *senikaladabagok* for a cough, *sagadaboak* for infection, and for the horrible, decimating smallpox, *ahamoakezenal. Anaskaweziak manhakwôgan* made a great poultice for a bruised, swollen lump. One older French ensign named Andre Regnault Miller (he used his full name) bought 'joe-pye weed' for gout. Zwame knew all their Alnôbak names, but the French could never remember them. So, she learned the new names, like 'goldenrod' (also good for a hacking cough), and used them interchangeably.

At times the family visited Odanak, which grew as war forced the Alnôbak from the east and Mohicans north from the Albany area. Though Wawanolewat and the Woronokes tended more to the south, along Bitawbákw, many of Bilinto's people were farther north, and the families visited from time to time. They also passed through Kahnawake, the village of Catholic Kanienkehaga, their houses perched above a fierce set of rapids on the Ktsitekw River. This was a good place to trade for strouds, the European cloth useful for a hundred traditional purposes, especially clothing. While there she observed Bilinto talking and joking with a great warrior named Athasata, sometimes called Kryn. Bilinto encouraged him to come to Chambly and throw down his war hatchet against the southern encroachment.

The French extended a standing invitation to all dawn-landers who wanted to ally with them against the British, and even managed a treaty with the Hodinohso:ni alliance in 1701. Some Mohicans decided to stay at Schaghticoke and fight for the English against their own people, and others went to stay in the Kanienkehaga villages of chief Sagayaeanqueprohton, who remained neutral. The dispersals of Mohicans were a mournful thing, and the Pocumtucks fared little better. Alnôbak and Pocumtuck warriors allied with the French frequently gathered colonists' scalps for bounty (as did the British and their allies), or took captives and ran them up to the northern territories, enjoying their colorful British difficulties along the familiar Alnôbak paths from the Mkazawitekw river to Onegígwizibó, or the Wôbitekw to the Winoskítekw.

Bilinto journeyed down and back twice during the summer with Wawanolewat. For her part, Zwame hated the travel, wishing instead to settle down for weeks at a time with Namito and her Woronoke family. Wizwame and Nebilinto had a daughter now as well, beautiful and smart, whom they named Gihla after the brave, black-capped songbird *kejegigihlasiz*. She toddled about, only four, but she seemed an ancient soul—a philosophical child, a wide pair of perceptive eyes at Zwame's hip, taking in the words and actions of others and thinking about them deeply.

As a grounded mother, Zwame much preferred her years at the quiet home near the falls to the villages near Fort Chambly, which were filled with French and strange Indian speech, as well as desperate, impoverished people moving from one misery to the next. In general, she hated living in this area altogether, as did the rest of her family. Still, she could understand most people well enough, and when word was spread that the French soldiers would hire English speakers to translate, she took the job, at five livres a month. Monies always proved useful in the French villages, and with steady income, her family could get by well.

She became acquainted with many of the British prisoners waiting for ransom or release in the purgatory of Fort Chambly, and they talked of many different things. The prisoners eventually grew to trust the white girl, and soon her directions were not simply to translate, but also to gather intelligence of colonial plans, and the military strength in different villages. Also, Zwame worked to assure the prisoners that neither the Catholics nor the dawn peoples could be judged 'savage,' as so many seemed to think (even the French referred to men as *sauvage*, and women *sauvagesse*, in their legal documents). As the French made a point of decent treatment of prisoners, they pushed the Hodinohso:ni and Alnôbak to keep their charges well. (Left to their own devices, the Alnôbak enjoyed threatening or humiliating their captives, for example making them sing ridiculous songs naked, or making them run a gauntlet of men, women, or children, who would beat them as they covered their heads, crashing down the line.) Hundreds of people moved through the garrison in the course of a year, and Wizwame witnessed all manner of foreign customs. She paid attention to the differences, and then tried to help new prisoners to feel more comfortable in their captivity—that was one of her jobs. Another was to argue points of religion with the captives, and win them over to Catholicism if possible. Zwame had little interest in this responsibility, but it became part of her banter in any case.

Two or three of the prisoners had lived in Hatfield. Once, talking to a middle-aged man named John Stockwell, he asked her "if she were Elizabeth Sackett, taken from Westfield in 1683?"

Apparently Benoni Stebbins of Deerfield had told people down river that Elizabeth Sackett still lived, just up the Kwanitekw from Northfield. Stockwell read about the Sackett child, and he had talked to Stebbins. A few months later a group of Koasiak took him near the Ashuelot, and he came to Chambly.

Zwame admitted, yes, she had been Elizabeth; no point in pretending the event never happened. She wondered to herself sometimes if someday she would go and visit these people, who had once been her parents. She wondered what it would be like— how unlikely it was they would ever bridge the gulf of time and culture. After this meeting, news of her identity spread quickly among the prisoners; they persistently called her Elizabeth, and encouraged her to visit her family. One nice man, Samuel Gill, actually charged her with the responsibility.

"Elizabeth, you need to see them, to complete yourself. Part of you was ripped away when you were small. Which you need to make yourself whole again."

"I don't feel any major loss, in this life," Zwame replied. "Your habits and religion were strange."

"Yes, even a few years here can cure a man of some of the more foolish practices. Ha! I remember all the children had to be silent almost all the time, back in Salisbury, and Sunday was positively miserable. Hellfire and damnation. I'm starting to see why you prefer it up here. But you still should visit your relatives, in a time of peace." Gill was more open-minded than some, and he was starting to fit in. He could be released in a few months, more than likely, and maybe he'd stay in Canada.

Her little boy Namito was six, rambunctious, and a joy to her family. He explored everything, approaching the world with wide-eyed wonder and an even temper. He slept peacefully at night—unlike Gihla, who flopped around and stuck toes in the small of her back. His brown hair flowed in soft waves from his head to his shoulders, and his cheeks still showed a puff of baby fat. Mostly he stayed home with his 'grandmother' Atahla. Bilinto and Zwame saw him in the mornings and evenings, mostly, now that Zwame spent so much time at the fort. Some days he would come along with her, and play in the courtyards where Zwame met. He cheered the prisoners, who didn't get to see children very often, and they responded to his young, male energy. They watched him running to his mother, laughing as she swept him into her arms, and it warmed their hearts.

"Elizabeth, that's a beautiful boy you have. What did you name him again?'

"Namito. It's short for *kawazinamito*, for his dark eyes. Namito, say hello to Mr. Stockwell."

"Hello."

"He knows English?"

"Only a few words. He can say hello, goodbye, and that his name is Namito, at least."

"He should know more than that. We should teach him more while we are here. We can do that much good for him."

"I would let you do that."

"I think he deserves a good English name to start out. Which it seems fitting that it should be one that shows his bloodline, since he has one. I'm going to call him Sackett." His tone was light, and he might have been joking.

"I don't want you calling him that. How about David or George?"

"David Sackett would be fine."

"How about "little Jacques?" She taunted him back, as the word "Sachette" could be translated that way.

"No French names, if you please!"

But these people languished here for months, and her efforts to avoid an English moniker proved a losing battle. In the end, the name Sackett stuck among the British prisoners, and after many months the boy answered to "Sachette" as well as Namito. Zwame hated to hear it; the name brought back distant, troubled memories. Somehow it felt worse to hear her child called that than she her old name, Elizabeth. Gihla somehow avoided these attentions; she had a way of remaining unnoticed, despite her intense awareness of everything that took place. The boy seemed to garner all the attention.

But she forced herself not to complain, partly because when she thought about it, it would be good for Namito to learn English. Besides, she held to her mission clearly, and remained loyal to her cause. Even when the other dawnland boys started calling him 'Saksis,' she said nothing to stop them. She could do greater damage to the British by forbearance, gaining the prisoners' trust. So her son had some new names. Many people had a lot of names. Finally, she and Bilinto had him baptized. Jacques Sachette. Saksis.

The French and Alnôbak authorities all agreed Zwame should convince these New English visitors of her sympathies to their interests, that she even harbored a secret desire to return to Massachusetts, to her family, and her Christian fold. The British were surprisingly ready to believe such preposterous notions. And allowing the prisoners to teach English to Namito would not only be educational for him, it would provide another excuse for her sit with the prisoners and discuss life in the towns north of Springfield. Over time, Zwame discovered that the colonists planned to push northward and build forts along the Kwanitekw, to protect future settlements in those areas. Deerfield had grown considerably in past years, and it seemed likely the soldiers and colonists would organize there before pushing north to construct their fortifications. On the day she discovered the colonists' imminent plan to push northward, she walked briskly to her father's tent, beckoning to Bilinto on the way.

$$\sim\!\!\sim\!\!\bigcirc\!\sim\!\!\sim$$

Wawanolewat took in the news of the forts with interest, listening to his daughter's explanations in the arched fur wigwôm he'd built himself of long posts made from small *winsak* trees, their flexible ends bound together in a sweeping parabola. The man's experience and strength emanated from his eyes, and the rippling muscles of his foreams. Now forty years old, only a single, grey streak remained at the widow's peak of his flowing salt-and-pepper hair. He carried prestige, regularly engaging in high-level discussions of military strategy as the foremost Pocumtuck leader. Now he was even considered a leader of Mazipskoiodanak. It made sense. Indians had to join together, or die.

Wawanolewat could never be friend to the Bostonians; more than anything would have liked the freedom to visit his home soil when he liked—now, he heard, the forests were razed clear as if an evil wind had pulled all the native trees from the earth, dried them for a few years, and set them ablaze, burning roots deep in the soil. Everywhere fences, houses and stone chimneys had risen across the land, changing it forever. He hadn't seen the land himself in a very long time, partly because many thought it foolhardy—partly, he just knew it would break his heart. Six years since he visited the cave in the great mountain where he and Malalemet brought little Zwame on their way to Schaghticoke, after they found her in Tomhamaucke, his childhood home.

For all these reasons, Wawanolewat supported the dawnlanders in their persistent, harsh treatment of prisoners on the trail north. If a Brit were made to toil on the trail, or lost a toe to frostbite, it were nothing. The black robes had explained that the British sins against the Indians were egregious, and their suffering on the trail north atoned somewhat for their actions. Wawanolewat, for his part, believed the colonists could never reach absolution. Still, British men were soft, and if they lived, they'd at least be hardened by the experience. Finally, they brought good money when ransomed.

Otherwise, he'd just as soon see them killed. Their population needed trimming. Some attrition on the trail would be a good thing; no one could deny they were breeding like flies. His grandfather had shared stories of Champlain on Bitawbákw—how he massacred the Hodinohso:ni, while the Mazipskoiak stared, unbelieving. No dawnland tribesman had ever considered that approach before—just killing everyone. But all things considered, maybe that was the answer with the British. If only it were possible. He was willing. He would do his part to get the job done.

He soon came to realize Zwame's value as a source of information, and through the Schaghticokes and the Alnôbak, along the trade routes and Bitawbákw, a lot of useful intelligence poured in. Finally, he sent Bilinto to tell heads of families and the French commander that they should gather for a council. In two hours, his son-in-law brought back word that the French would host them for dinner that evening at Fort Chambly.

The wooden fort protruded on an outcropping of the Richelieu River, which flowed from 'Lake Champlain'—just a little farther north, at Sorel, the Richelieu met the 'St. Lawrence.' To Zwame and her family, the Richelieu still flowed from Bitáwbakw to Ktsitekw, but they learned the new French names. A hundred years before, Champlain himself had come and shown the Mazipskoiak a new way of life (including the unabashed massacre of enemies in open combat). Now the French had new names for everything, it seemed, and a pretty strong-looking command of the Ktsitekw.

That evening, a diverse group of natives met in the clearing before the fort. In addition to Wawanolewat and Malalemet, who represented Pocumtucks, two Mohicans attended, recently arrived from Albany, with simple clothing, and single feathers in their hair.

One heavily tattooed Kanienkehaga arrived with them, both sides of his head shaven, and a neat line of hair extending from his forehead to the back of his neck. Then there were fourteen Alnôbak, including Nebilinto and another Sokwaki, six Mazipskoiak, two Penecooks, two Pigwackets, and two from Koasek. A Micmac warrior hailed from the eastern islands. Then, ten Kahnawakes, along with their priest, Father Nicolas. The Kahnawake, being Catholic, declared themselves allies of the French and Alnôbak against the British. Their leader, Athasatam, announced their intentions. "We Kahnawake stand before you ready to do some damage to the colonial dogs. We hate these thieves with a furious passion." Three Hurons from Lorette came as well, including a chief and a well-respected warrior named Thaovenhosen.

Together the thirty-odd men walked coolly into the fort, smiling to themselves at the fear they could sense in the French guards who witnessed their confident and imposing presence. They met French commander Frontenac and Capt. Jean-Baptiste Hertel de Rouville, resplendent in blue woolen uniforms with crossed white bands, gold buttons and feathered triangular hats, flanked by lieutenants and ensigns who shook hands and offered greetings in various languages.

A Kanienkehaga stood with him already, a Catholic convert originally from the northern Adirondack mountains, and one from Mazipskoik, who worked as a translator. The group seated themselves leisurely in a large circle in the room with a crackling central fireplace, and chickens and meat were passed around. People dipped cups in large bowls of water. Discussion flowed, and opinions in favor of action were generally of a piece.

Wawanolewat began with explanations in Alnôbakiwi, the ordinary Mazipskoik speech. His voice resonated, and a French translator echoed his words in the background as he spoke. "Good men of the dawn people, our friends, and our hosts, welcome. My daughter Zwame has determined from the English prisoners here at the fort that there are plans among the British to push northward on the Kwanitekw, and establish footholds in the traditional Sokwaki and Koas lands, including territory where my family lived before coming to this village, following the generous invitation from our French allies. My son, Nebilinto, belongs in the Sokwaki woodlands.

I have travelled far—I know all this land well, and it is not difficult to repulse the British as they begin their colonial efforts. But I would not like to allow them to establish fortifications, as that would make them much more difficult to attack. Now, there are villages south of Sokwakiak, on our old Pocumtuck lands where our fathers hunted, easy to strike—isolated and unprotected, the colonists are easy targets in their wooden houses. We have struck repeatedly and successfully against them over the years, driving them out of Northfield, and attacking them at Hatfield and Deerfield, below the beaver tail. There, we will strike again! Hard."

Wawanolewat's voice grew in strength and conviction. Low, deep, serious, his words exerted powerful influence on sympathetic ears. "For this mission, I rename this village. Guerrefille, daughter of war. This new group of militia, it is said, will organize in Guerrefille and strike out from there in the springtime, hoping to begin their work before the new leaves have begun to show. We need to determine a plan of action now. We should destroy them."

One of the Mohicans spoke next, in fluent Mazipskoik Alnôbakiwi. "We have come from Schaghticoke, traveling two long years now since we left that town in turmoil. Everyone would control us there—during our long stay in Albany, the New York governor Cornbury wanted us to stay and fight for him, and we also received secret invitations from the French to head north to join them and fight the British. Most of us had lost our stomach for these wars, and seeking safety, left to join the Kanienkehaga, with whom we have had peace in recent years, and whose neutrality offered us better sanctuary. Peter Schuyler tried to stop us as we left; he offered foolish lies, saying the British would protect us and care for us if we stayed. As if they didn't bring destruction on all our people, and left us all in refugee camps, where once we had forests and flowing streams, *mowômagok*, *mozak*, *belazak* and *wôbimenal* to the roof! As if they didn't poison our lives with their foul ideas and their incredible arrogance!" Murmurs of agreement spread among the assembly. "We told him what we thought, and went on our way. We met with the Kanienkehaga further north, and while some of us stayed there, most of us have moved to French settlements. But it is our understanding that if we strike the Massachusetts settlements, the Hodinohso:ni would not raise a hand against us, and possibly, New York would not either. Relations between the two colonies are not what they were." The Kanienkehaga with him nodded in agreement. "So we cannot promise many men; but we do bring news of your insulation from reprisals from the West." The crowd smiled its relief, and lapsed into animated side conversation for a few moments.

The Penacooks were next. "River Indians were sent by the British Earl of Bellemont to us with wampum belts, offering a similar request to join the British alliance at Schaghticoke. They found a similar response to that the good Mohicans here offered Major Schuyler. We heard nothing of their poison council. We are few in number here, but we stand with you against Massachusetts Bay Colony, which spreads like disease. Ossipees, Winnapausaukees and Pigwackets will join us as well."

Father Nicolas, representing the Kahnawake, addressed the convention in French. "Good people, our enemy is your enemy, and our mission against Guerrefille holds great purpose for our community. We understood that our church bell, which we so greatly desire to install in the belfry of our church of Sault St. Louis, was lost to a British privateer, en route to Montreal. The story is a sad one; through our long labors, we laid aside a portion of our furs until we had enough money to send to France for a bell, through a representative we sent to Havre. Our bell was carried upon the barque Grande Monarque, toward our community, which so greatly desired it. However, this New England privateer took and brought it into the port of Salem, where he sold it as a lawful prize—to whom? The church of Guerrefille! The very town which sits like a blood blister," and he turned to face Wawanolewat, "on your Pocumtuck heartland. You will find our Kahnawake community desires greatly to return this bell to its original destination. We will serve in this campaign with special dedication." Many Kahnawakes shouted their support, and it took a minute or two for the noise to die down, as others cheered the warlike spirit on.

The leader of a group of about twenty Hurons spoke simply, briefly. "And the Hurons stand with you." The hardened men looked grim. Hertel de Rouville stood to seize the moment, and summarize the general situation for the entire assembly.

"People of the dawn. Our Catholic friends, and apostolic allies." Rouville addressed them through his translator, and gestured toward the Alnôbak and the others as he spoke. "Governor Vaudreuil feels we would benefit from a great alliance, to strike at the heart of the British colony in Massachusetts. There is much to understand about mother France's motivations in this war. We have a new king in Spain, one of our own, a Bourbon of the house of Louis the 14th. As you know, we are at war. We have heard of the gathering of forces in Guerrefille. They plan to take your land, settle and rape it. You know what they do, and how we all hate them. We should kill them together!" The people nodded and murmured loudly in agreement. "Also, there is a man we can take whom we may ransom for Captain Baptiste, the great privateer—captured almost two years ago, he's held in Boston, and our allies would benefit from his assistance and his spoils. This man, a preacher and politician, is named John Williams, now living in Guerrefille. If we take him, Britain will want him back. They will trade for anyone we ask. We can free Baptiste."

Rouville went on. "We will plan, and wait until the winter

is on us, and they are weak, and travel more difficult for them. Your people have a great woodland advantage over the foolhardy British colonists, especially in late winter. Then, we'll destroy their town, and kill and take as many as we can. Even if they mount an organized pursuit, we'll leave them far behind, with plunder and captives. We'll return to Chambly in glory!" From all corners, men whooped and hooted assent.

And so the growing confederation generally agreed to strike the Massachusetts colony during the coming winter at Amiskwolokoi, the heart of Pocumtuck land, the village now called Deerfield, or Guerrefille. The floor opened to everyone, now the leaders had spoken, and individuals proclaimed support and pledged supplies and men. Wawanolewat, his grey hair and muscled, lanky frame appearing weathered and strong in the firelight, offered his services as guide and war sachem, along with Malalemet. When the party dispersed some time later, the men went home to explain their plans to friends and family, and begin preparation. Much of the talk at the fires was of captives. The elders, and especially the women, clearly embraced the opportunity to grow their communities a bit.

The word Mazipskoiak (as well as the name Kanienkehagak) meant "people of the flint." Just south of the village nestled an excellent chert quarry. The Indians had two months to make arrows, knives and tomahawks, string bows, sharpen steel blades, clean firearms, gather ammunition. Women fashioned snowshoes, pounded dried *skamonal*, mended the men's *mozal* robes, prepared them for their long, cold traverse. Skilled hands made many extra winter moccasins, knee length, fur-lined, designed to be worn on top of regular moccasins, which were also lined with fur. With centuries of hard experience behind them, no one shod their families better in winter snow.

Wawanolewat convinced Bilinto, with some difficulty, not to come along. The thought of their family losing all its men weighed too heavily on him. Zwame naturally joined in this chorus, and eventually, Bilinto was convinced. Atahla was unconcerned; used to this coming and going to war over the many hard years she had spent with this Woronoke clan chief, she trusted him to come home. This family business complete, Wawanolewat traced the benefits of a successful battle with his family.

"If we destroy Guerrefille and sew fear along the northern settlements, they may not try to settle further north for many years. Then we should be able to get out of this town, and back to the woods, closer to the lands where our fathers hunted."

It seemed an intelligent approach to everyone. Bilinto missed the home along the brook, his Sokwaki homeland. He voiced his agreement. "Namito will grow up wrong in a town like this. There are too many bad men in Chambly. We should get back to the land, and good hunting." The boy hung on his father's knee as he spoke.

Atahla, matriarch, spoke for the family. "We have made friends here. But this place is thick with French coldness, and European thinking. We need more children to learn the Woronoke ways. Also, we cannot thrive in a place like this. Zwame's work is hard on her—they pull the strings of her old life, and we want no part of the European ways. We work with the French because we hate the Bostonians more. Much more. But when we can, we should leave this place. As soon as we can." Her words were true for all of them, and no one wanted to follow up with counterargument. It was agreed that after the brothers returned from battle, the family would move to Koasek, along the northern portion of the Kwanitekw. That should give them room to be themselves, to renew their traditions, and stay well clear of the British, over two hundred leagues to the south.

That night, a dream brought Wawanolewat to the western shore of the Kwanitekw. He stood in a quiet, snowy place, looking around in peaceful meditation. He looked across alluvial sandbanks at the mouth of a tributary, and then saw the forest to the south burning, consumed by an uncontrollable blaze, suddenly rushing toward him. He felt hot wind, smelled the smoke, and soon the entire shoreline across the way raged in orange glory. Out of the smoke, crashing through the trees, he saw two metal monsters, breathing black steam. He knew they would poison the river, and kill all spirits living here. He watched, rooted to the spot, as their steel teeth devoured the burning forest, and animals fled the destruction. He felt protected by the icy river before him, but across the river was an horrific sight. His eyes jerked back and forth under his closed eyelids for a long while, taking it all in.

Early in the morning Wawanolewat traveled back to the physical realm—his body awoke, he and his brother geared up quickly, and when the force of two hundred, mostly native men assembled at Fort Chambly stood ready, they set out on foot pulling a few small sledges. They traveled along the edge of Bitawbágók, and often directly over it where ice reached firm across the inlets. Many knew different routes to the Kwanitekw, and the leaders decided to follow the Winoskík river up into the highlands and across to the Wôbizibo river, where they descended to the Kwanitekw just south of Koasek. The hike wore on, long and cold, challenging Frenchmen who couldn't get used to the temperatures, and shared their discomfort by complaining constantly. "*Tabernacula*! You *sauvages* are inhuman! How can you stand it?" The Alnôbak grinned openly at their weakness, and their foolish clothing. Other than a few scouts who also served to hurry the ranks along, the natives let the Frenchmen go in front, to set the pace. Some already had frostbite and lost toes by the time they made it down to the Kwanitekw. Again with the foolish European shoes. They built fires along the river, and regrouped a bit before heading south.

The huge war party hiked vigorously down the long stretch of water, and the effort proved arduous and cold. At least they could usually travel straight down the frozen river, instead of the uneven riverbank. They made pretty good time. When they reached the mouth of Wantatstekw after two days, they halted, set up lookouts, and had a war party. Their fires burned brightly that night, and stars were crisp and clear. The travelers ate relatively well—mostly *skamonal* meal, their staple, and a good number of rutting *mozak* the hunters had been lucky enough to come across on the Ktsi Mskodak below the falls. Malalemet and his grey-haired brother had stopped to gather two caches of *wobimenal* from up the brook, just a mile below the meadows. Compared to what the men had been accustomed to on the march, that night the small army ate like kings. Still, they'd split the meat and nuts two hundred hungry ways, and in the morning they had to bury a number of *mozak* carcasses for their return trip, deep in a snow cave. That evening, at a fire circle of twenty men, Wawanolewat rose and spoke clearly.

"Brethren, dawn peoples, listen to me. I am of the beaver, and the beaver is this land. Temakwa. Once a great pond welled here, and a giant beaver lived in it. It cut the trees and dammed the water, flooding part of the house of the giant Hobomuck, and he laid it low with an *anaskawezi* trunk, right here. The animal sank, and turned to stone, and now the water is almost gone. When you stand atop the mountain here and look to the south, you see its foot and tail across the river, stretching to the south. The tail rises just above where the Bostonians planted their houses, and further south, the head rises, just east of my homeland. Our ancestors, they said that. They made that. They wanted it that way.

What we do at Guerrefille, we do for the Sokwaki and the Pocumtuck people, whose fathers hunted here. The largest Pocomtuck group is the Amiskwolokoiak; they lived right here, below the beaver's tail. Many of you are sons of this land. Others are our brothers from the north, who share our hatred of the white culture. What we do tomorrow, we need to do. We should have done long ago. But we do it now, and it will be done.

I have seen in dreams the burning of these lands; the poison these people bring. These people are the toadstools, the destroying angels. An invading fungus on our precious earth." Murmurs of approval went up among the gathered people. Wawanolewat called out, "Not long ago, our friends and relatives were treated evilly by these people. None of us remembers the massacre by the Hodinohso:ni at Fort Hill. But is there anyone among us who remembers the Great Falls massacre from the time of Metacom?"

Two hands went up. "I was supposed to be there. I was late. I am alive only because I stopped to rest upstream, at Fort Hill." The greying man sounded sorry about this, as if his presence could have saved his family from death, and if not, it would have been better not to live.

"A good thing you were not there." A younger man, maybe thirty-five, rose as the crowd hushed. I woke to my grandmother and sister, terrified. I ducked out a side flap even as men ran into my *wigwôm*. I heard my grandmother scream, and my sister. Their voices just went out, like someone had grabbed their throats—they were so loud, and then nothing. I ran into the night, a small child alone, and in two days made it to people I knew up in Sokwakiak lands, along the river. That night comes again and again to my memory. I will do some revenge, to help appease the spirits of my sister and grandmother."

One older warrior spoke up. "We paid them well for our horrible loss. Some eighty of us collapsed on their troops from positions both north and south along the river, and killed many. I killed ten. Word of their depravity spread through our ranks, and we were enraged. I saw Turner die, and we drove Holyoke south, driving them into a corner, where we finally left them."

A teenager, painted red and black for war, called out, "You did well, old man. Tomorrow we kill more!"

Other stories and statements fell along these lines, and one Kahnawake spoke in an impassioned manner about their anticipated recovery of the church bell. Then the men slept well, with thoughts or dreams of revenge. In the morning, they carefully arranged their supplies, stashed them, and began a stealthy but vigorous march down the river on snowshoes. The weather had warmed a bit from what they had been used to, and the snow was damp and sticky. They spent that night at Sokwakiak among the niwaskok—the spirits. No one stirred at the Northfield palisade, which seemed abandoned. Ghosts of the Sokwakiak and a few colonists drifted in the mist. During the night, everyone could see their forms reaching out, fingers spreading, mouths calling silently. Many men did not sleep very well, and everyone stayed close to the fires. Wawanolewat stayed awake, encouraging the spirits down toward their enemy, to keep them awake—and so the morning of the raid, the villagers would sleep soundly. He did not fear these wandering souls, and when he lay down in his warm clothing, sound sleep came at his bidding.

At dawn the pack of men trudged on, and at dusk the next day the troops hove into sight of Guerrefille. They hunkered down for the night, lying together for warmth. This time their rest felt pretty successful, on the whole, though it turned out to be a colder, windy night. Before the morning came, a hard crust lay across the surface of the snow, just enough to carry a careful walker, without breaking through. They stashed their snowshoes. With his instepped, careful toe-ball-heel step, Wawanolewat led a long string of men across an open meadow, painfully aware of the noise their march made behind him, a constant, quiet crunching across the surface. To avoid notice, he had the men run forward with the gusts of wind, then stop and listen when the breeze tapered off. They met no opposition, set off no alarm, and soon the troops arrived safely at the edge of town, just behind a ridge at the northwest quarter, looking down at the village. Their cover was perfect. Wawanolewat spoke to Nivervilee. "Sir, this is the best possible situation. We command over two hundred well-armed men—forty-eight French, and 160 dawnlanders. This sleepy town is ours for the taking."

Niverville replied, "And so it begins." He sent the order down the line for a charge, double time, and at his signal the lines moved across the open fields like three rogue waves, colliding in a foamy sea.

Wawanolewat and Malalemet went left, leading their flank; his men proceeded in well-organized fashion, fierce and merciless, with groups of five attacking each house, and twenty for the central buildings. Upon clearing a house the war party moved to another, and when the houses were all raided, they rejoined the main force in the center of town. For their part, a large detachment from the center column had orders to take the main town buildings, and then hold prisoners that the groups of five brought back for them. Burning, pillaging, and general destruction were the order of the day, and few of the invaders neglected to observe these details. Some foolish people put up an impetuous fight, sometimes still in bedclothes and bellowing oaths; the men shot or tomahawked these fools straightaway, and took their scalps. As for brighter men who threw up their hands in surrender, ran, or huddled in terror with their families, the warriors tied their hands and sent these new prisoners to the town square by the church, under guard. Many young children who could not make the journey were put swiftly to rest, and the weaker men and women. A group of smarter men tried to organize resistance;

French soldiers, focusing their fire, cut them down swiftly. Their houses then had only women and children, easily emptied and sent ablaze. Not much of a threat, though many of the war party were wounded, and some killed in the process.

The northern army thus set the town afire, and brought nearly all its citizens to utter defeat and captivity. Men reveled in their bloody work, and the town reeked, warm with burning. A few houses were left, partly because the heat was too intense to bear. The used one to collect captives, and when they brought in a dying Frenchman who called out in thirst, the matron, Mary Catlin, offered them water. She treated them well, and they left her and her house untouched. Many of the prisoners were red, later that day, as if sunburned. The impressive assembly grew, some surly, some resigned, some in terror, some stricken with loss of loved ones. One house at the southern end did stand, a two-story log building with a particularly fierce set of occupants, and after several attempts to take it, the soldiers decided to leave it be. The name on the door was Sgt. Benoni Stebbins.

Wawanolewat and his brother stayed together, in the center of things. Their large group took the main fort with ease, and soon prepared to burn the church, which, they knew, firmly condemned their cultures. Many of the French had been baited by name-calling Protestants; they hated these supercilious, self-righteous followers of heretical fanatics like Calvin and Zwengli— acting as lofty as if God himself had sent them, and they were Christ's own brothers. Some of the Frenchmen had been called "dirty Papists" in their time, and bore the Pilgrim god no love. The British were hypocrites: subjugating anyone and everyone they could; massacring these poor dawnland people indiscriminately, and seizing their land; dominating the cod industry along the coast; and encouraging privateers to seize French ships laden with furs, and kill French sailors, or imprison them, as they did Captain Baptiste. And they believed, without hesitation, they were pious followers of the true, rigid path of God. Yes, greedy hypocrites, the British were, and extremely dangerous.

To all the Indians, the Protestant steeple in the sky represented a spearhead of arrogance and devastation. British used the steeple to jab the sky, and justify their land-grabbing myth of *vacuum domicilium*, whereby 'apparently unoccupied lands should become theirs—theirs to put a fence around, cut down all the trees, and declare forever their lawful property—to which an aboriginal, territorial Wôbanakiak, whose fathers had hunted on that land for generations beyond memory, had no claim whatsoever. They would all enjoy its destruction immensely. Prior to firing it, Father Nicolas exhorted Rouville to send two men up to ring the bell.

Minutes later, a clear, single peal rang out in the village. All fell silent as its tone washed over the raiders and prisoners alike. It seemed to carry great power and message, in the dramatic moment. The Kahnawake were absolutely spellbound. Father Nicolas called out, in French: "Men of Sault St. Louis! Let us claim it for our own!" Ten of them entered the church, brought down the bell, and with great effort carried it carefully to the central rallying point, and stood around viewing it, waiting for the soldiers and warriors to finish their work. Fired by the memories of their lost land and people, their many close relatives starved, killed, or dead of illness, the invaders killed fairly indiscriminately and cut off every scalp. Most took no joy in killing women or children, rather gathering them as prisoners, though some did, remembering British massacres, knowing they would be paid for extra scalps, just as the British soldiers were. The priest Williams, his family, and anyone who looked prominent were rounded up and marched to the meeting place.

After taking the fort and the church, the brothers set to breaking down the door of a house adjacent the church. Bursting in, they found a man pointing a pistol directly at Malalemet's chest. He fired, and the gun merely clicked in his hand. He proceeded to shout obscenities at the brothers in a loud and barbarous fashion. The brothers threw him to the ground, tied him, and stripped his clothes off for a while to teach him some manners, while others pushed past them into the house. Wawanolewat saw one of the Kahnawake killing first one child, then another, and he called out in protest. Already, a black woman, different from the others, lay dead in the pantry. Five more children were brought out, along with a feeble looking woman. The Indians tied their hands and marched them all outside, where other bound prisoners were gathered. The sky grew light, but remained grey and overcast.

In the end only about fifty colonists were actually killed, while over twice that number were taken captive. Most of these regarded the natives and French in horror—sad, forlorn faces, fully expecting to die presently in a gruesome manner. A group of Mazipskoiak killed one infant on the spot, deeming him too small to survive, indifferent to his mother's stricken protest. Then, as the early morning sun rose in the sky, they forced prisoners to run north, along the river at a speed they would not have guessed possible. Most of the prisoners had been poorly shod, and the dawnlanders stopped to replace their ridiculous shoes with moccasins and snowshoes. Father Nicolas and the Kahnawake, endeavoring to bring the church bell, hastily rigged some poles to carry it.

While doing this, they were attacked by a small group of resolute men from the south, who suddenly appeared on horseback. The men dropped the bell, and ran out the other end of the fort. They raced across the open pasture for the trees. Rouville pointed a few soldiers at this group, and called for an immediate retreat. He sent an order to kill all the prisoners prior to the withdrawal, but as the messenger ran across an open area, he was shot and killed. A few more minutes skirmish, and the small group of British scampered in flight. Rouville realized they were not in immediate danger, and luckily for the prisoners, countermanded his own order. As it happened, a few Indians who had no interest in dragging these weak people northward—and remembering the British massacres of their own people—were inclined to kill all of the captives. Rouville prevented this, encouraged by Wawanolewat and others, who remembered their families' desire for new tribal members. But he did order that the bell be left behind.

The Kahnawake seemed despondent. A few other Catholic dawnlanders shared their depression. Engraving on the bell showed it was indeed originally intended for Sault St. Louis. Quickly, they covered it in branches fifty yards from shore, due east of a small island on the river.

They finally set out on the trail northward, pushing the captives to run. Many could not keep up, and the army did what they could to help them, but if they didn't manage, they were killed. In the first few hours, soldiers along the row of prisoners struck down five people, dispatching them quickly with powerful blows to the back of the head with a hatchet. Witnessing loved ones and neighbors dying in this way, the remaining group spurred itself to greater speed, and they kept up the pace all day until they reached a large meadow maybe ten leagues to the north.

There they encamped; the dawnlanders made branch houses to protect everyone from the light, oppressive sleet that began to fall. They bound the most athletic of the prisoners, but even still, one escaped. Others, they knew, had escaped from the scene of the attack, and they presumed that soon a detachment of soldiers would be pursuing them from Hatfield or Northhampton, and their very lives depended upon the speed of their retreat. Men murmured among themselves. Maybe there was a large garrison just south in Hatfield who would head immediately north, hearing the news of the attack, and overtake them, better armed and supplied, and destroy them all! This was a nagging fear, oft spoken. The more experienced had some confidence that no detachment of Brits could cover the ground they'd managed overnight in that weather, and arrive in shape for battle. Wawanolewat smiled inwardly at the thought, and amusedly at anyone who suggested concern. He knew, and he told them. "Not a chance."

At first light the sleet fortunately ended, and the army set out like a pack of frightened rabbits, driving the prisoners forward in their midst. The warriors carried many of the smaller children. Just after leaving the camp, they needed to cross a stream, and someone fell in with a splash—the feeble wife of the man who tried to kill Malalemet. She clambered to the shore, cold and dripping, and struggled to climb the hill on the other side. She slipped and fell, and appeared injured. Her husband bellowed at his captors, insisting they let him help her. Instead, an impatient Mazipskoi ended the argument by burying his hatchet in her head. Though the man whined throughout the day, they did not kill him as well.

Their collective, relentless pace seemed painfully slow through the rest of the day, and another young woman and an infant were killed at the rear of the line. As the dusk came on, they arrived at the edge of the highlands that signaled the beginning of Indian territory, and they camped in one of the sheltered alpine swamps which had a good view down the river. Many of the dawnlanders were becoming annoyed with John Williams, the loudly complaining prisoner, the prize of Governor Vaudreuil, who would bring a large ransom to the Alnôbak. The Hurons, who had lost their chief at Guerrefille, decided they needed to kill Williams to avenge their leader. They began to, but somehow Rouville caught wind of it and begged them not to; apparently this man would be a valuable prisoner for the French, and a principal objective of their mission. Still the Huron were set in their minds, and many would not be dissuaded. "He must be sacrificed," his nephew said, "in expiation."

A warrior named Thaovenhosen disagreed with his fellow Hurons. Whether his motivation was merciful or mercenary, he stood bravely in favor of sparing Williams' life. "Hurons, people of Lorette, hear me. I pray you will remember you are Christian, and this cruelty does not become you. If we do this, moreover, the Hurons will be disgraced in Quebec."

"I, also, am related to that Chief whose fall in battle we mourn, and whose death you would avenge by unworthy cruelty." Thaovenhosen continued. "To me also is the captive due; I claim him as my own, and I contend that such is my right. If anyone lay hands on him against my will, let him look to me for chastisement."

Thaovenhosen was a scary warrior, perfectly deadly in battle, and all among them knew it. The crowd grew silent, and Williams was saved, though he was little aware of it.

At the end of the next day they reached the supply cache at Wantatstegok. They sat huddled for a few long and painful hours of darkness. Hastily constructed sledges pulled some of the weaker prisoners, so the killing could be lessened. The large majority of soldiers and warriors generally felt that the threat of chase from British soldiers, whom they had not found at Guerrefille, was very real. Morning found them already heading north up the thawing Kwanitekw; the two Woronoke brothers went ahead, and when they reached the brook where Namito was born, they turned to the west, up through the shale ravine and across the swamp, past the stone face, to gather a large cache of *wôbimenal* and *anaskawenal* from the circular root cellar, among the hickory and *wôbimiziak* trees which stood black, wet and welcoming in the thaw. The day turned to a cold rain, and the snow grew heavy, with ankle deep slush buried under feet of wet snow. The broken crust scraped like rough blades at the brothers' legs as they returned to join the large group. Many captives complained of frozen toes. The pace remained very fast, and Indians dispatched many prisoners.

"The Bostoniak not in good shape. Many will die before they make it to Chambly. We should bring some furs." Malalemet had been practicing his English, which still seemed very broken. He did not enjoy the prisoners' discomfort in the wilderness as much as some others.

"Very well. We'll take the last two caches of nuts, as well. They'll all need whatever we can offer."

Thus, when the Woronokes arrived at their former home, they gathered the remaining supplies they had stored about a year and a half before, just in case. They uncovered the bundle of fur blankets, neatly rolled and stashed in a rocky outcropping, and covered with a stone. They were in excellent condition. Then, they uncovered the buried nuts, and put them into sacks they had brought, along with a light sledge. Next they put the bundles onto the sledge, and turned their backs on their former homes and the lovely little brook. They talked further, exchanging memories as they crossed through the white drifts of the tall *koasak* grove.

The brothers caught up with the procession easily, as it made hard, slow going into the evening, and the entire group finally reached the Ktsi Pôntekw, exhausted. They established a quick camp, with blankets and people huddled in piles, sleeping only if they were capable. Others merely took a few hours rest. It was fairly warm, which decreased prisoners' misery in the night, but kept the troops worried they would be captured easily by soldiers headed up river, following their massive track.

"*Dalizogwebaso*," Malalemet said to his brother at first light. "The ice is breaking up." They could see huge, white chunks moving slowly on the river below the falls. So at first light, the prisoners were roused, given a handful of corn, a place to drink, and then forced nearly to run up the soggy snowbanks of the river. They immediately protested, saying they could not possibly keep up the pace, and they must rest and eat, or die. So it came about that soon after leaving the falls, the large group stopped briefly to regroup by an inlet, and the brothers passed roasted *wobimiz-iak* nuts among the prisoners. During this pause Williams stood and addressed his fellows, praying to his God, reading from his black book. Wawanolewat knew he had found an appropriate passage—the man said it was "from Lamentations"—and among his oratories was a portion that read "Behold my sorrow; my virgins and my young men are gone into captivity." But the warriors had little patience for this sort of thing; there was no way of knowing if soldiers were behind them, or how close, and all could so easily be lost. Soon enough the drive continued forward, mercilessly. Williams was relentless, constantly berating the warriors near him, who regarded him dispassionately. He used all sorts of derogatory names.

Williams had four children: Samuel, fourteen; Esther, thirteen; Steven, nine, and Eunice, seven. The two youngest could easily be brought into a dawnland family; the party treated them with special care along the trail, carrying Eunice much of the way, or putting Steven on a sledge when he couldn't walk.

That day wore on inexorably. Warmer weather led to wet clothing, and hungry and exhausted, a few prisoners fell, and couldn't go on; their skulls were quickly crushed and scalps gathered along the way. During five more days of hard travel, six more lagging prisoners had been killed. The ice was unsafe, and the long string of well over three hundred people had to keep to the uneven shoreline. Many of the Alnôbak and the few Pocumtucks knew the routes well, and led the army along narrow but unobstructed paths over the hills by the river. At times when the packs separated, they slid messages across the river ice, rolled and tied to long sticks. A strong heave could put a heavy stick clean across the river.

Finally, they reached the Wôbitekw, and there the retreating army finally relaxed, to spend some time gathering food and resting for the return journey to Canada.

It appeared that some of the others had similar thoughts about traveling to Koasek, at least to visit it, because many broke off to join a small group of Koasiak who wanted to travel northeast further along the Kwanitekw to Koasek after a couple of days' encampment at the Wôbitekw. Rouville liked this idea, finding it difficult to provide for such a large party, and encouraged them to separate, suggesting that many of the group could continue north from Koasek into Quebec via the Winoskík.

It seemed logical to Wawanolewat and Malalemet that they should head directly to Koasek to gather wood, build a house, and ready the earth for crops. They arranged for close friends to deliver the message to their families, to join them as soon as they could make the passage. After some final time hunting, and gathering any other food they could come across, the main body of soldiers began a long march over the cold mountains to Mazipskoiodana.

The preacher Williams continued with the large group, and the two Woronokes were not sorry to see him go.

"He is merely a tool of the British." Malalemet, said, fed up with Williams' complaints. "Maybe the French will kill him on the way."

Wawanolewat saw a bright side. "His daughter seems okay." He'd thought he'd seen some disdain at her father's noisy protestations.

"Yes, she's a keeper."

Their detachment, heading to Koasek, had little food—just the bags of ground *skamonal* which all the Indians carried, and some *apenak*, which they rationed off meagerly to the Guerrefille townspeople. Still, they felt liberated, setting off with about forty Indians and twelve of the captives, two of Williams' children (including the girl Eunice), and two nearly starving men named Holt and Hix. The smaller group followed the Kwanitekw away from the larger pack of people, and their collective needs. They'd be better able to provide for their captives, they thought, and when they arrived in Koasek, at the tall *koasak* of the upper Koas, they'd stay and prepare a home; they women would be happy to see it, when they finally arrived. In a few weeks, when the prisoners were well, Wawanolewat sent them to Mazipskoik, under Malalemet's protection. He would return with some wealth, to last a number of years—payment for their valor and leadership, measured in scalps and prisoner bounties.

1713

The weather began to change. Low thunder rumbled along the west side of the ridge, as Zwame paddled with Bilinto and Namito below the Ktsi Pôntekw and past the brook, heading down to the Sacketts in Westfield. Ten years since Wawanolewat had passed north this way, coming from Deerfield. Twelve, since she had seen the mouth of the brook, and the massive canopy of *koasak abaziak* spreading above it. She remembered how time passed from the Deerfield attack onward.

"Look after them. Find out what they know about encampments and reinforcements. Anything planned for the future. Well-to-do families in new, northern settlements who might build a blockhouse, and host a garrison." The directions from the self-important Lieutenant Daneau De Muy were clear enough, and they'd pay five livres a month.

Working with the prisoners at Fort Chambly seemed flat, dull, and cold during the weeks after her father and uncle left for the attack on Deerfield. The British were strange creatures, and though a very few seemed good, modest people, such as Sam Gill, she learned to loathe most of them utterly. As a result, she began to avoid the place, preferring by far to spend her time playing with Namito, helping her mother and aunts with the diverse work which kept them all going. Endless basket weaving. Sometimes they bartered for goods, and sometimes they bought supplies with the money Zwame managed to bring in. Her husband Bilinto hunted daily, and often brought some animal in for dinner, like *magôliboak* or *bakesoak*, and sometimes food for days, like *nolkak* or *bagoniak*.

Once during midwinter, he managed to drag home a massive *moz* on a makeshift sledge, and this led to a feast like none other that year. Colored leaves and dried flowers were hung from the walls of their domed wigwôms, and the families ate festively, enjoying different specialties the women made from the internal organs, and whatever else they had to contribute to the feast—dried mushrooms, *skamonal* dishes, *apenak, wasawal.* They missed the brothers, gone on the Deerfield raid, and worried about them. The wind blew frigid, but in well-sewn, furlined clothing, the large family stayed cozy and mostly happy.

When the warriors returned safely with the large collection of prisoners, the women were overjoyed and ran to meet the Woronoke brothers—but they did not find them, instead discovering they had gone to Koasek to prepare a new home for them all. Good news! Deferring their longing to see the two men, they packed and left Chambly. In a period of weeks they arrived in Koasek, finding a new home well underway, by the headwaters of the Kwanitekw. A few miles away they could see the divide, and noted where the water flowed north toward the Ktsitekw and Odanak.

As the brothers anticipated, the women loved their new wigwôms in this beautiful place, far from the crowded Richelieu; the whole group stayed for four years. They had to hide from colonial soldiers in the first early summer, when a group of Bostonians had suddenly appeared, surprised and killed eight of the Koasiaks, looked around, and left. The family had time to make it look as if they'd left in a hurry, for good, even though their fields were newly planted. But when the colonists headed south, they simply moved back in and continued to tend their silky harvest of *skamon.* After that season, they headed further up river, well above the village, and lived there a few years among other Koasiaks.

The band of western Alnôbak was good people, and the ancient, towering *skamonal* in the intervales reminded Zwame of the Great Meadow near the stone chambers where she bore Namito. Their new friend, the energetic Father Lauverjat, described it as a *"cathédrale de pin blanc et le jaune."* Namito passed eight winters before they moved to Koasek, and when they left he had known twelve—a wiry child with long brown hair, the same deep brown eyes as his mother, and an acquired, native sensibility regarding the land. Little Gihla's years there were very healthy. She learned extensive herblore from her mother and her community, as well as basket weaving, cooking, how to make clothing, and speak many languages. She showed a fascination with the complexity of different people, and tried to understand everything she could about each new person, and cultural group. Besides her brother, all agreed she listened wonderfully, and remembered details.

The bow of Zwame's canoe pointed south, and she passed the Ktsi Mskodak now, intending to stop on the return trip to show Gihla their former home. From a sandy cliff, *benegôkihlasi-sak* dipped and swerved in and out of their sandy cliff-dwellings as she passed slowly, floating and paddling along with her family in a well-crafted *maskwaiwigwaol*. They kept their strokes clean and crisp, their backs straight, and their hands out over the water. When the water picked up speed, they planted the blades in the water and went with the river, riding the eddies, crossing the tongues of water at an angle, then easing up when the water grew calmer.

For the past few years their Koasek home nestled on the south side of a foothill in the ancestral Alnôbak region due south of Odanak, where the springs of the Saco, Androscoggin, and Kwanitekw started in the mountains, just to the north. Now they lived just west of Mazipskoik, north of Winoskík, in a new, palisaded village her father's men carved out of the woods.

Wawanolewat had become a celebrity over the years, having been involved in more raids against Western Massachusetts than just about anyone, with the possible exception of his brother. In a large celebration held in Mazipskoik, attended by most of Winoskík, the Alnôbak made him a chief. He was getting on, now about fifty years old, and he'd decided to establish a stronghold on firm ground. His entire family and a number of friends' families joined him in constructing a village within a log enclosure, and they all settled in comfortably in this permanent-feeling home. Pole by spiked pole, they palisaded the settlement.

Atahla smiled. "Nice arrangement." After thirty years separation from her homeland, she approved of the enclosure and its battlements. Maybe the next generation could live more than a decade in one place.

Well attended by women in her wigwôm, Atahla had her last child a few months later, baptized Nicolas Ouaouënouroué. They called him Noluwey. Even as Wawanolewat prepared for more attacks, he felt peace in his heart that this child had a stable place to live; a much more promising childhood than his own in the cauldron of Woronoco.

"He has a strong, clear gaze." Wawanolewat liked to hold the child and look into his eyes. The infant and elder traded expressions by the hundreds, making tireless faces at each other.

Dedicated to their role of keeping colonists at bay, the villagers remained happily embroiled in bloody, vengeful excursions way down the Kwanitekw, and they even joined some eastern Alnôbak in an invasion of Haverhill near Boston, via Wiwnibesaki Nebes. The fight came near to them a year later, though there was no real threat—a group of fifteen British soldiers and two Mohegan fought a band of Kahnawakes on Bitawbákw; the invasive troop led the Kahnawakes into the woods, up the Winoskík. A mistake. Along the way, the detachment ran into his brother Malalemet and twenty others escorting prisoners from a small Deerfield raid. The invaders rounded up quickly, surprised Malalemet, and attacked immediately; they almost managed to cut out a prisoner. Malalemet defended well, and his men spread out on two flanks. Deliberate fire killed five and chased the rest of the British off, south and further west, scattering into the woods. The dark came on at that point, and after chasing them into the wood for a couple of leagues Malalemet let them go, figuring they'd get lost.

Complex events led to the Treaty of Utrecht, and from far away the agreement brought a temporary peace among most of the English, French and Indians. It boded unwell for the eastern Alnôbak, though—as part of the treaty the French king ceded Acadia to England, in exchange for the installation of a Bourbon king on the throne in Spain. Wawanolewat, ever connected with the bands of refugees coming through Koasek, consequently refused to acknowledge the treaty despite the strong French ties of his people.

Zwame enjoyed quiet family life in the village, but after the peace in 1713, she and Bilinto decided to head east and south again to visit her birth parents. The Sackett family figured in many a long campfire discussion since her meeting with the two colonists in the majestic *koasak abaziak* grove on the great meadow, and she had grown more curious, and less afraid over the years. Wawanolewat was able to tell her many things about the Westfield homestead—he knew John Sackett in better days, before Metacom's alliance in the 1670s. Zwame relished the idea of seeing their reactions, when she met them with her Abenaki husband and fifteen year-old boy who kneeled in the bow, his stroke a crisp J, while she worked on some new moccasins. Bilinto served as the rudder astern, while Gihla sewed the three-flap footwear with her mother amidships.

In the canoe, they traveled easily through Deerfield and marveled at the strange experience of passing openly through British territory. Though many watched them intently, at first no one bothered them. The low, rolling, manicured hills, and the flat, wide, treeless fields of the Pilgrims appeared strange, after long experience in the heavily forested hills and valleys to the north. Occasionally, the pilots of various small boats came near to them on the river, asking, "hello, who are you?" and "can we help you?" Nosy and unfriendly, was the family's impression. Zwame invariably pretended the busybodies had asked after their welfare, and replied: "We are well: how far is Northampton?" Their canoe eventually came into the great oxbow, revealing a wide, swinging river, a beautiful plain and to the east, a prominent crag of rock, clearly part of the Pocumtuck beaver. Planted, manicured farm fields and fences abounded. Cows roamed over wide fields, and large farms sprawled with pigs and chickens near the barns. The land became mostly flat, for miles around.

They arrived presently at Northhampton, where she left Bilinto and Namito by the river and walked up toward the center of town. People made eyes at her dress, and along with her blonde hair, she was obviously a captive turned Abenaki. She walked quietly to the fort and addressed an important-looking, round-faced man with black, woolen clothing. "Many years ago, a John Sackett lived here in town. Now I think he lives back in Westfield, where he'd come from. Have you heard of him?"

"Indeed," he replied, "a John Sackett lives still in Westfield, on land he's kept a generation and more. Girl, how do you know the man? What business have you with him?"

She looked at him a moment. "I'm his daughter." She smiled slightly at the wide eyes she received in response. She turned, and walked briskly away, down to her family waiting by the river, idly fishing. They were happy to travel on, away from the town, down the last, long stretch of river. They slept that night way downriver, below Springfield, comfortable in a stand of trees by the bank. No one bothered them, but probably only because they remained quiet and unnoticed.

They had to paddle upstream on the Woronoke (now Westfield River) for three or four leagues, but it wasn't bad, really. The treelessness felt strange and unsettling. Lines of well-spaced trees marked the borders of land, but otherwise, there was precious little forest, except on the tops of the dramatic hills that towered over the river valley. Zwame couldn't imagine too many animals making their home here, except on the hilltops, or in the barns.

It proved a long stretch of river, and in the village communities, people stared at them as they went by; they were getting used to that. Namito observed puffy, pale faces, and felt most of the adults looked unwell. The children mostly looked wide-eyed and silent, very different from the laughing packs of young Wôbanaki up at Winoskík. Some of the adolescents looked resentful, as if they'd recently been told not to do something. Namito felt smug, knowing he preferred his life to theirs.

"I wonder what they do for fun," he mused.

Bilinto offered, "Probably not enough. They seem tightly dressed. The cloth looks course. I bet they spend a lot of time reading their Bible and finding things to do that won't get them in trouble. On Sundays, they probably just lie around. I heard these people don't work on Sundays." He regarded them as strange and curious creatures, worthy of study, if only they weren't so deadly. So systematic in their destruction of land and people. There were still many things about his wife he didn't fully understand.

Zwame explained, "It's their Sabbath—their day of rest.

When their God made the world, on the seventh day he rested, and so do they. I have vague memories of extreme boredom, and then everyone working very hard all the rest of the week, and nobody saying much except in a severe way. They always seemed to think I should be doing something I wasn't. My memories are few, and hazy—I remember images—a wood floor, wood chairs, a thick wood table. My mother sewing, in a white apron and a simple dress. My father's gun over the door. My sisters and brothers sleeping in the loft. My own rope bed, lumpy and uncomfortable, very small. The night I was taken by Wawanolewat." She continued, gazing into space. "I remember feelings, too—feeling bad a lot, like I had done something wrong. Feeling good, seeing my whole family at the dinner table. Wonder, when my father said grace, listening to his descriptions of the power of God. Thinking about God seeing everything. Fear, at night—fear of our people. Funny, that. I guess it changed for the better! But since then I learned fear of the colonists, the people I came from. Now I don't fear them anymore. I want to see what my parents have to say, when they see me. I want to see my brothers and sisters."

"It will be good for you to see them. It may not be a happy experience for either of you, but I'm glad we go." Bilinto seemed sure of himself, as usual. She felt his reassuring strength, his steadiness.

Her son's motivations were different—she had wanted him along, and he agreed, more for the adventure than because he was interested in any long-lost family connection. Immersed in the Alnôbak world, he couldn't imagine living differently. It seemed unreal that these were his mother's original people. Gihla, on the other hand, seemed prepared to learn everything she could about these strange new relatives.

They made good headway against the current, and in the early afternoon they approached Westfield. Neat, split-rail fences separated homesteads neatly, and patches of corn and wheat grew in large rectangles.

When the family arrived at the riverbanks of Westfield, they hid the canoe in a stand of *bakwaaskol* and walked together up a brush-covered bank through a young forest of *alnizediak* and *koasak. Pezagwdamenakwamak* brambles grew thick in many places, and old, ancient hardwood stumps rotted here and there. They passed through the scrubby patch of woods, and out onto a road leading toward the middle of town.

Along the road, they met a man driving a wagon, with a horse. He smiled at them as he rode slowly along. Zwame asked "Does John Sackett live in this town?"

"The older, or the younger?"

"The older."

"Why yes, I should say he does! One of the first colonists! Follow this road through the center of town and turn left at a fork a few rods further along. You'll pass two farms. The third one is Sackett's. And who would you be?"

"An old friend of the family. Thanks for the directions." She didn't want them to find out before she arrived, and she was sure the Sacketts wouldn't want the town to know right away their savage daughter had returned. People might tell them anyway, but at least they wouldn't know for sure it were she until she saw them.

She didn't have to worry. They came through the middle of town in ten minutes, and another ten minutes later they came upon the third farm. It looked vaguely familiar—the house had grown, a new barn stood in the yard, and the open space had grown—in fact, the panorama was unobstructed, except for a few stands of *senemozi* and *wôbimiziak*. Really, I don't recognize a thing, she thought. An older man stood, chopping wood. Around the side of the house, a woman hung washing. Zwame knew, the way you know an old friend from a distance, only stronger. It was her family. She continued walking up the road, much more nervous now. The woman saw them. Bilinto held her hand...they all knew. Then the man looked up.

He took them in for a full minute, a good, long look. Then he knew. The maul fell over, and lay on the ground. He called out, "Elizabeth?" The woman looked over from the billowing laundry, and let out a short, choked cry. She walked over, looking happy and shocked and horrified, all at once. Staggering a bit.

"Elizabeth?"

"Hannah. Father." She had decided to call them mother and

father. But her mother did not appear.

"Oh my dear God, child, my God. Lord among us. My God." Her sister's breath was short, and she stopped about six paces in front of her sister, and stared, hesitant. Tears formed in her eyes. She ran forward and embraced the young woman, suddenly sobbing. She didn't let go right away, but held her close for over a minute, releasing her racking sobs into Zwame's chest. Her father stepped up, and stood close. He did not offer to embrace her. He stood there, looking at the three dawnland people.

"You speak English?"

"I never lost it, really. I met a woman who spoke good English soon after they took me. I've been able all my life."

She went on. "This is my husband, Nebilinto. He is a very good man, but he doesn't speak much English. This is our son, Kazawinamito. Your grandson, I guess. We just call him Namito. And this is your granddaughter, Gihla." Discomfort hung in the air, as the Sacketts regarded the strange visitors. Hannah broke it by inviting them all into the house. They followed her in and sat at a thick, wooden table. John came in last with a slight limp and sat in a large chair by the fire, facing the table.

Hannah spoke freely. She seemed strong and outgoing. "We heard you were alive. Only fifteen years ago—before that we thought you were probably dead. Since we heard, we oftentimes wondered if we'd ever see you. It is good there is peace between our people now."

"Yes, the peace makes travel possible on the Kwanitekw. It is strange for us to be in this world, the world of the colonists. We are used to the Wôbanaki ways. Bilinto works hard. Namito is a great hunter, a very responsible young man. My life is entirely fulfilling. But I wanted to see you."

"We're glad you did. We thought we'd never see you again." Her father's eyes were damp. He managed to broach some questions she longed to discuss. "I guess I should be glad the savages brought you up safely, and kept you alive. It's hard to give up your child, though, and I don't think I can really forgive them. You do understand that, don't you?" He looked at his daughter for a few moments. "What happened to you? All those years." The weight of separation lay between them.

"What do you want to know? It would be hard to tell you everything."

"That first night. Do you remember? How did you get by, and what did you go through? Then, where did you live? I've thought so much about that night. We all did. Wondering."

"Well, I do remember it, some. They carried me, and we did some running. It seemed very far, and I was very scared. They treated me well though, and sometimes we stopped and rested, and the land was beautiful. I played with crayfish. The men were amazing...they could do so many things. They were kind to me, which seemed strange because I missed you so badly. They didn't speak English for a few days. Then a woman who spoke English came, and explained things to me, and told me that I would live with them. Which was up near Schaghticoke, in New York, a busy Sokwakiak town."

"I knew you were probably in one of those holding pens. We thought you might be in Stockbridge, and we sent word to have them look for you at Fort Massachusetts. But we heard nothing. You were just gone."

Hannah spoke up. "I'll never forget that night. That Indian came in—just looked at us girls. Big man, long black hair, with a white patch on the forehead. Not afraid, not threatening to kill us. Just looking at us. Looking around. Saw you, walked over, and picked you up. Looked at us again. We were frozen. He ran out into the night. I was so sad, I loved you so much."

Zwame changed the subject. "What about yourselves? What has your life been like?"

"I'm married now," Hannah said. My second husband, actually. Ben is away, stationed in Hartford, Connecticut—he's a soldier. I stay up here with father and the kids—Child is twenty-three, now, and then there's little Marah." The four-year old girl watched them silently from a chair in the corner of the room. "I've lost two boys."

"I'm sorry."

Her father explained, "Your mother died about ten years after you left. We wandered up the river for a while, looking for you, sort of. We had to tear down our dam here in Westfield—court order—and I was having a hard time making ends meet. There was work there, and we thought we might hear word of you up that way, where the raids were happening at towns like Deerfield. You people weren't involved in that, were you?"

"Of course not. We were up to Canada then." Zwame sensed it might be a bad choice, to boast of her other father's exploits here.

"Canada?"

"That's where we're safe. Chambly is rebuilt now, after it was burned in your year 1709. We usually live near there. Down here in Woronoco and other Pocomutuck areas, your people took a lot of land, and killed to get it. You have to admit it."

"Which there's been enough killing on both sides." John remarked. His heart was just softening after the initial, hard confusion, and now he was inclined to change the subject. "Your boy looks well. He looks strong. You've done a good job with him." The Sacketts were apparently not as prejudiced as some. "You say he knows some English? How about he and your husband come and look around the farm with me?"

"I'd like that." Namito was quick to reply. He found the place fascinating—he had seen henhouses up in Chambly, but this was his first New England farm, and there was much to see. He marveled at the cozy barn with two horses and two cows, nestled snug in clean hay. He said to John, "They look happy."

"I expect they are. We like things clean and fresh in here. The cows are all milking. Have you ever had fresh milk?"

"Not from a cow. From sheep."

"Sheep's good, too. But here, try some of this." He took a clean mug from a small cupboard near the door and eased over next to one of the cows, stroking its side. He pulled up a stool from behind him and took a teat in one hand, clamped off the top and squeezed. Milk shot out onto the floor, and then he held the cup under the stream, which filled it quickly. He held it out to Namito, who took and drank it all.

"Mmm, that is good. Can my father have some?" John filled the cup again, and they passed it to Bilinto. He tasted, and smiled, and drank it at a draught. Namito said, "Are there wild cows in England?"

His grandfather laughed. "No. And come to think of it, I don't know where cows come from originally, or if they were ever wild."

They toured the paddock and looked out at the fields of skamon, and the garden of herbs, beans and squash. The two Sokwakiak felt better outside again, in the warm, open air. The garden flowered beautifully, and warmth started to develop between the two men and the teenager, despite their differences.

They stayed for a week, building a small, arched wigwôm in a patch of woods close to the Sacketts. On the fourth day, Hannah had a conversation with Elizabeth (she allowed them to use her old name) and Gihla at the kitchen table while the men were out hunting.

"You know, Elizabeth, when we lost you we tried to find you. When we couldn't, we had to assume you were gone forever. So we could move on."

"I understand."

"No, I don't think you do. I haven't said what I mean to say. When we decided you were gone—I don't know how to say this— we declared you dead. Legally. I guess we didn't want people to think we had an Indian daughter. Besides, we thought you were probably dead. The Indians killed a lot of children in those days. They were savage people, showing no mercy."

"You know of the colonists' massacres, don't you? The Pequots, Penacooks, Sokwakiak, and all the others? Killing women and children?

"Yes, but that was war. Killing women and children? I heard of some families dying in a raid up at Turners Falls, but I don't know about the rest. I knew there were attacks and battles between the English and the Indians—so many, ever since I've been alive! It's a hard life."

"No, sister, it's been worse for my people than you can imagine. That raid at Turners Falls? Shooting defenseless old men, women and children in their homes, where they'd come to gather fish. People everywhere pushed out of their homelands, killed and threatened when they visit the lands their fathers hunted. Before the big push of British colonists, disease destroyed our people. It still destroys them. We were so many more you can't imagine, with wealth and ceremony and civilization. But disease laid us low, and ruthless land-grabbing people wipe up the mess of our towns, and drive us north and west to towns in Canada, seeking refuge. Never think our fight is unjust."

Hannah actually winked at her. "I'll try, but considering I lost my five-year old sister after savages burned my family's barn in the night, it's going to be difficult."

"Well, we'll take it slowly. I am glad to see you again." The sisters embraced. Hannah gave Gihla a warm smile, and held her hand, showing she accepted the darker-skinned girl as her family, her own niece. Gihla positively beamed.

The next day they dissembled their makeshift *wigwôm* and headed south on the river again. Beautiful hills and cliffs along the Woronoke became farmland, and soon they turned north on the main stretch of the Kwanitekw, with its flat land all the way up through Whately. At the Ktsi Pôntekw they stretched on the rocks, enjoying the natural beauty of the jagged, mica-schist streambed, the river cutting a magnificent gorge. Faintly yellow flycatchers dipped and swooped above the stream, hunting insects. In the trees, they called out—"*bvrt. Fitz bew!*"

Namito leaned over a pool and watched the flashing bodies of *skotam*, hanging in the current. He slipped his hands gently, slowly, into the cold water, and reached out as far as he could, and waited.

Slowly, one of the softly swaying fish drifted above his fingers, with careless flicks of its tail, riding the powerful current. He tickled its belly slightly, and as it relaxed, he quick-flipped it through the air onto the bank. It lay there gasping, iridescent green scales spotted with shiny rings around black spots. Namito caught two more in this way, then took his knife from its sheath and cleaned them. By this time, his mother had a simple fire going in a small pit.

They ate well, finishing with berries and a good chew on a golden birch twig. They stretched by the fire and fell asleep.

Gihla rolled, in a dream. She sat up in the darkness, her head spinning, woozy. She saw in a sliver of moonlight the black water rushing through the land. She was able to leap forward and glide in the water, riding it quickly from the mountains, streaking like an underwater arrow up to the Ktsi Pôntekw. But instead of leaping the stages of the falls as she anticipated, she swooped up against a massive wall. Again she leaped high, fell helpless, back into the lower pool. She swam around the face of the wall and surfaced. The water was deep, a massive pool, and after checking the rocky corners (it seemed she could breathe underwater), she finally found a place to wind through, toward the river valley below, which she longed to follow. She swam a narrow, winding path through a building, over hard, uncomfortable objects. She came up into a horrible pool of pushing, bumping fish—massive, flailing, dead fish. Silver, crammed, stinking. Suddenly she couldn't breathe, couldn't surface. Voices screamed around her, and a massive weight pressed down on her chest. She couldn't open her mouth. With incredible effort, she came out from under the smothering and gasped a terrified breath. Her eyes popped open.

"Little Gihla, what is it?" Her mother's voice came softly, right by her side.

"I saw the river stopped. *Mskwamagwok* died in a tangled clump, hundreds of them. Thousands. I couldn't breathe."

"You dreamed it. It felt strong?"

"Yes, overwhelming." She curled up against her mother, and they spooned in the warm evening, under a blanket. Eventually, they slept.

On the way home they stopped to visit the stone chambers where they used to live, and the cathedral stand of *koasak* at the Ktsi Mtsodak. Gihla stood silently at the old camp for a long time, taking everything in. She delighted in the carved stone face her mother showed her, which reminded her of the sun, smiling at her with puffy, radiant cheeks.

Carrying the canoe around the second falls offered a happy exertion for Namito and Gihla, who both felt young, strong, and grateful, with a lot to think about. Along the way they watched the birds, and learned more of their names—the *benegôkihlasizak, ceskwadadasak, medawihlak,* all manner of colorful *gwigwigemok. Mozak* dipped their noses in the water, and *temakwak* played on the river, swimming in groups at the first and last light of the day. At the Mkazawitekw river, they parted.

Bilinto headed west, past Ascutney, to rendezvous with Wawanolewat in Mazipskoik, while the mother and her two childen traveled the Kwanitekw up to Koasek, and stayed a few happy months with the friendly people of the *koasak* intervales, abounding in *moskwasak, awasosak, mskwamagwok* and *mozak, megezoak* and *azebanak.*

1723

The early sun dawned as Wawanolewat and ten able warriors poised, like sharp-eyed buteos circling above a farm in Rutland, Massachusetts, watching every movement of a man and his three sons skillfully raking and coiling hay with pitchforks in a quiet pasture. The twisted straw mounds were a thing of beauty.

For ten years, peace reigned predominantly between the French, English, Hodinohso:ni and Alnôbak. After King William's war most Alnôbak lived in Mazipskoik and Odanak, with a few in Schaghticoke, or, like Zwame's family, on the Kwanitekw above Koasek, or near Memphremagog. Since the big European treaty in 1713 there had been little conflict. Still, unlike the others, Wawanolewat would never sign a treaty. He would remember forever the injustices that the Pocumtucks, now a refugee people, had suffered during the colonial invasion. A few years after the peace was settled, he began to leave his stronghold near Mazipskoik with small bands of carefully selected warriors to visit colonial settlements in the Connecticut valley to wreak havoc once or twice a year. His chosen recreation kept him spry and resourceful.

Now sixty, he stood strong and healthy; he traveled fast over the rocky ground of the mountain passes. With this older age came an almost adolescent sense of recklessness—if he died while punishing British settlements, what difference would it make, since his life was nearly at its close? But his recklessness never showed inexperience. He was braver than ever, but also wilier, with a carefully honed sense of strategy, with which he employed fifty and more volunteers gleaned from Mazipskoik, loyal to the dawnland cause despite the Treaty. He often thought how sad it was that he might die, with Bostonians still residing in Woronoco and other Pocumtuck lands. There was much to be done, and this year, opportunities for action came again and again. Besides, his time would come when the spirit-world had a need for him, and not before.

Early in the spring Lieutenant Governor William Dummer tried to broker a peace treaty with the northern chiefs. He managed to gather considerable support, especially from the Penobscot Wenemowet, whose people were vulnerable. Dummer really wanted a pledge from Wawanolewat, whom he called Gray Lock, as colonists called him in the Westfield area in his younger days; for decades, the name struck horror throughout the Kwanitekw watershed. Wawanolewat relished the notoriety. The governor sent wampum, tobacco, pots and pans up Bitawbákw, and offered to prevent colonists from moving north on the Kwanitekw if he'd agree to stop persecuting the northern settlements. They didn't have a proper wampum belt, though, and the Mohican messenger seemed worried about that detail. Truly, it didn't matter in the slightest. Dummer could move a granite riverbed more easily.

The Kennebek River Alnôbak had seen a very hard year. The good Father Rale, whose extensive notes on the Alnôbak language were the closest thing to a dawnland dictionary, was butchered at Norridgewock with thirty men, women and children. Though a medicine man's vision warned many people, motivating a hundred and fifty to depart safely, the remainder nevertheless withstood another brutal massacre. Both the human and property losses, the Penacook people and the ancient village, severely lacerated the whole community. On a flyer posted all over Mazipskoi-Odanak, the Jesuit Charlevoix described the situation:

Warned by the danger by the cries and tumult, Father Rale went fearlessly to meet the assailants, in the hope of drawing all their attention on himself alone, and thus saving his flock at the peril of his life. His hope was not in vain...although more than two thousand shots were fired at them, only thirty were killed and fourteen wounded. The Indians immediately returned to their village, and their first care, while the women were seeking herbs and plants proper to cure the wounded, was to weep over the body of their holy missionary.

They found him pierced with a thousand blows, his scalp torn off, his skull crushed by hatchets, his mouth and eyes full of mud, his leg-bones broken, and all his members mutilated in a hundred different ways. Thus a priest was treated in his mission, at the foot of a cross, by those very men who on all occasions exaggerate so greatly the pretended inhumanities of our Indians, who have never been seen to use such violence to the dead bodies of their enemies.

A hundred fifty refugees limped into Canada, and settled mainly in Odanak and Bécancour. Nanoudohout, principal chief at Odanak, made them feel welcome, and organized groups to bring food and supplies and to begin building *wigwôms*.

The people were angry.

The French still refused to enter the war, but many, upset at this latest atrocity, encouraged the Indians as much as they could. Wawanolewat and Onedahauet, along with fifteen other men, discussed the matter with Frenchmen Beauharnois, Aubrey, and LaChasse, who argued for patience. The Alnôbak would have none of it. They scorned Dummer's British puppets, and instead sent Wawanolewat's brother Malalemet with a separate belt to symbolize rejection of the offer. Further, they directed him to New York, to see if Yorkers would raise a hand in the defense of Massachusetts. They suspected no love was lost, and the Yorkers would allow them to proceed freely against the Pilgrims.

Remembering the Kanienkehaga massacre at Sokwakiak, Wawanolewat remained concerned about this, but also felt hopeful that territorial politics would prevent New York's involvement. Based on the indications his brother received in Albany, this was the case, though the Yorkers tried to discourage them from their little war. It appeared moreover that Massachusetts endeavored generally to recruit Hodinohso:ni to fight Alnôbak, which attempts were fortunately unsuccessful—in response, three well-spoken emissaries from Masipkoiodanak visited Hodinohso:ni clans to ask for peace between the dawnland peoples, and they were able to talk things through. The Hodinohso:ni sent word to the British that war would set the governor of Canada against them, "and that would set all the world on fire." They considered this a foolish and destructive alliance, and consequently rejected it.

So Wawanolewat and Onedahauet felt the strength of their position. Dummer's weak attempts at diplomacy made them contemptuous of the British—remembering lies from the past, they were certain they held the power to continue attacks without much fear of serious reprisal. And so in the high summer they'd resumed their insurgent campaign against Northfield and other towns, enjoying fast runs up Onegígwizibó and down the Mkazawitekw and Wantatstekw rivers, or else up the Winoskík and down the Wôbizibo. Wawanolewat wanted to push eastward, to hold back the flood of strange, violent, unreasonable pale-faced people who cut down the forests.

The stealth required in navigating the largely cleared settlements added excitement, a challenge for his well-trained warriors, gleaned from among the best in the greater Mazipskoiodanak area. This past run had seen mostly warm spring weather and a few days of misty rain, with an even longer period of grey stratus clouds blanketing the skies. The sun had come out yesterday afternoon for the first time in a week, as the men carried their maskwaiwigwaol around the Ktsi Pôntekw and paddled past the old *koasak* on the Great Meadow, and then the remains of Fort Hill, down below Wantastekwatso, now merely a ghostly river-bend covered in *pabalakok* and *majimskikoal*.

They slipped into the woods at dusk and fell on a farm in Northfield, killing a farmer and his wife in front of their house. Then they headed southeast by the moonlight; by daybreak they had traveled forty miles, crossing the wide and frothy "Miller's river." They crossed over an easy hill pass, and then followed the Ware River through the woods, with Mount Wachusett looking down on them through the daybreak hours, silently approving their work. The ridge by Deerfield provided cover, as few colonists lived near the great rock, the *temakwa* paw. The group stopped in the morning to catch three hours' sleep in the shade of a shale ledge, on the north side of the ridge above Rutland. When they woke they looked down at the farmers like goshawks viewing rabbits in the field.

Joseph Stevens stood in the field a moment, watching his four sons forking up and twisting hay. They were pretty good at it, except for Isaac who was not quite ten, and still ran around playing more than working; but that was entertaining to all of them, and it was a beautiful day. When the Indians came running swiftly across the field toward them, he didn't even see them until they had crossed a quarter of the distance, as they started silently. When the boys started yelling, the Indians whooped. Joseph panicked and ran behind a stand of low evergreen trees to the pond, and slipped below the waterline, using a reed to breathe. It was an idea he'd had many times in the days of King William's war, though he hadn't needed it. He didn't stop to see what became of his sons, though he thought about it while he was underwater.

The attack fell, swift and deadly. The two oldest brothers were immediately killed as they tried to resist. A third, sixteen year-old Phineas, ranged close to Isaac, and threw down his fork as he ran toward him saying "Just put up your hands! Don't try and fight!" The two horror-stricken boys put up their hands and stood numb, waiting for possible death. Instead the men tied Phineas' hands, and the brothers were told to run with the Indians, as fast as they could, into the woods and over the hills.

"Munch!" They marched.

At the edge of the field they ran pell-mell into a man, and Phineas called out "Run, Reverend Willard!" A quick blow from Wawanolewat's club dispatched the weaker, older man, and the group moved off again.

As he jogged along, Wawanolewat studied his club, regarding the smooth round stone bound tightly to the crook of a hickory handle with strips of leather—the beautiful, well-oiled wood grain, dark brown and smooth from handling. This had come from Woronoco, a gift from his father, while Wawanolewat was still a teenager.

Phineas' muscles had never been so sore. And though he was

a teenager, his heart suffered its losses. He had seen two brothers killed, and his father abandon them all, to save himself. He
struggled to imagine what it must be like for Isaac, just nine
years old, now bouncing on the back of the tall savage in front
of him.

Three days of hard running, taking turns carrying the small
boy along the Ashuelot (past looming Menonadenak) brought
the men back above the Kwanitekw, looking down from the ruins of Fort Hill. Wawanolewat took pleasure in their work. He
had actually allowed the older Stevens to get away. If the man
recognized his grey lock of hair, and they connected events, the
whites would have to fear a group of warriors who could strike in
Northfield one afternoon and then in Rutland the following day.
Above the Wantatstekw, they rescued three canoes from a thick
shell of brush, and paddled steadily upriver.

They hoisted the canoes around the Ktsi Pôntekw and set
them back in the water, stepping in lightly, and helped the boys
into the middle of two separate canoes. They paddled a short
way up the Kwanitekw, and turned off up the Mkazawitekw—in
another hour, they stashed the canoes well up the river, where it
turned too rocky to paddle. From there they made good time past
Ascutney and down Onegígwizibó to Bitáwbakw, where they followed the banks up to their large, carefully hidden canoe, which
could hold all of them together. They had to carry it a mile down
the hill from its hiding place, to a narrow inlet on the lake. Two
days later, they were home again, coming into Mazipskoik.

On the way into town they met a group of Kahnawakes, visiting to discuss a possible alliance against the English in the mari-
times. "*Kwai*, Wawalonet." The leader of the group had known
the Woronoke chief for many years. "Coming from the south-
lands?" He eyed the prisoners, and smiled. "You brought these
men from the Kwanitegok? We could use this young man here."
He indicated Isaac Stevens, who had no idea what the men were
talking about.

Wawanolewat appreciated the opportunity. "You want the
boy? We know how helpful your people have been to us in the past.
I have not forgotten fighting side by side with you in Deerfield.

Yours would be a valuable alliance for me, for all the Wôbanaki people, against the British plague. The boy is yours, in hopes of your friendship." He signaled to the men in Isaac's canoe, and they traveled toward the shore along with one of the Kahnawake canoes. Departing the group, his head hung low, Isaac was separated permanently from his brother Phineas. Wawanolewat headed back into his village with a few Kahnawakes.

There they visited, and regrouped. They left Phineas in Mazipskoik with Onedahauet. Soon Wawanolewat's crew headed south again, preferring to strike while the weather was warm, and during this season, they were not alone; other small military groups began to form in Odanak and Bécancour, planning and executing raids on the Massachusetts frontier.

His group headed south again along Bitawbákw, fifteen warriors strong. A line of four canoes, they paddled out into the glassy center of the lake one calm morning, passing through pickerel weed and some tiny, swirling gnats on the way. They had journeyed a day and a half, and they saw number of canoes along the way paddled by Kanienkehaga or Alnôbak travelers.

The boats drew together as they approached Odzihózo. One of the Kahnawakes spoke.

"This is a place of power. If you are willing, I would like to hear your people tell about this great god."

The Masipkoik, Amareguened, explained the story.

"We tell these tales in the winter time. Since you are my friend, I will share the knowledge with you. Long ago, a great being carved the landscape, moving around with his upper body and his arms, because his legs were very short. He dragged himself around gouging the rivers and piling up the mountains with his hands; where he sat, he left deep depressions, and when he moved he created trenches with his bottom. The water followed him in from the ocean, and kept coming. Legs sprouted on him like the tails on a tadpole, and he lifted them and placed them on the ground, making tributaries to the rivers. He made the great lake Bitawbákw, and impressed with his own work, he settled down where he was and turned to stone to observe it forever. Here he sits before us—Odzihózo, the One Who Made Himself. Our old ancestor, he said that. He made that. He wanted it that way." The group pulled up on the north shore, silent, and left a twisted plug of tobacco near a clay pipe that lay on the rocks. They felt grateful for light winds, and smooth paddling. Even so, out on the big water they needed to crouch low, and keep the bow pointed into the waves.

As they rounded the great rock they saw a detachment of New York militia in bateaux hove into view, rowing up from the south. These men eventually hailed them.

"Hello! Abenaki? Where away?"

Feeling safe from this distance, a Kahnawake yelled back.

"Ahoy! To hell with you, white eye! We have not quarreled with the Yorkers, but we will destroy Massachusetts!"

Wawanolewat bade him "Be silent!" and scowled. "Our brothers should not yell out our plans to the world."

Wawanolewat looked hard at the Kahnawake brave, who shrugged, annoyed. The comment rubbed against the dawnland tradition to boast of exploits planned or accomplished. Clearly, the old man set a high value on stealth, and above all, success in the mission.

They passed on, and soon they cleared the split, rocky cliff of Zôbapskwák and headed up the Onegígwizibó. The narrow, wooded and rocky paths seemed to whisper them along swiftly, as if the group itself were a mountain breeze. Down they swept to the Kwanitekw, using canoes stashed many leagues up the Mkazawitekw; they portaged around the Ktsi Pôntekw, and paddled south a ways. They set up for a few days near the meadows, by the old stone chambers, up in the hardwood forest above the *koasak abaziak*. They preferred ash branches for fires, to reduce smoke, and burned only at night. During the third day they received intelligence from a lone Koasiak traveling upstream, that Governor Dummer had warned the colonists of impending attack. They could expect that their adversaries would be hunkered down, alert.

Feeling safe in this little nook well above British settlement, the group spent another two weeks gathering *wôbimenal*, *bagônal*, and *anaskawenal*, and storing them in the old hiding places. Then, they gathered their weapons and stooped down the Kwanitekw to strike in Northfield.

They poised in the brush near one fort and waited until the doors were open, and half the people emptied out into the fields. The raiders had three muskets, but began with arrows—the bows were well made and reinforced, and at sixty feet could punch an arrow right through someone's midsection if the point didn't hit a bone. Bows were quieter. Three men fell immediately, and as they went in a fourth charged; one of the Kahnawake dispatched him quickly, knocking him to the floor and cutting his throat, with a knee in the small of the man's back. They found no one else there. Looking around, they found some supplies and two more muskets, along with balls and powder, which they gathered up. The group moved on toward another small fort they knew of.

Here over the crest of a hill, a man and an adolescent boy came into view, crossing the field in front of the fort. The gate stood open. The Indians ran toward them immediately, and caught up with the two. They shot the man in the chest as he ran toward them wildly, after seeing he had no chance of escape. The boy fell to his knees in helplessness and grief, his jaw working silently as his eyes bled tears. They quickly tied his hands, and ran into the fort. They found no one else there. That was well enough, they thought, and headed back north in their canoes, with the young captive, whose name turned out to be Samuel Dickinson.

"*Munch.* Move." Wawanolewat's voice carried no plea, and an absence of friendly encouragement. It was an order. They boy began to jog, fearing for his life. The troop moved along, ahead and behind him. They entered the woods quickly and quietly.

Apparently the Indians had caught the colonists completely by surprise, and no reinforcements appeared, as they half expected. It was a relief. Up the river they traveled, to the Mkazawitekw and over the mountains, down Onegígwizibó, up Bitawbákw. The boy was in good health and traveled well, and didn't give any trouble, though he looked sullen and said hardly a word. He was slow, like most—Wawanolewat struck him on two occasions, telling him to move along faster. Back again to Mazipskoik, where Wawanolewat kept his settlement some distance from the town center. The boy he sent off to Chambly, where he would languish until he was sent back to the English. Marching with his new captors through Masipkoi at the end of a long winter, young Samuel Dickinson noted Wawanolewat's newest war party, already seated in a circle. He stared silently as he strode past, and Wawanolewat met his gaze.

≋ ◯ ≋

For the dedicated warriors, spring's journey south was smooth and beautiful. The mountains rang with birdsong, and the band of twelve warriors watched a huge *moz* and *wôboz*, eating quietly, solitary in the wild, sloping pastures. Snow lingered in the mountains, and the changes in scenery and temperature were often dramatic, depending on the earth and sky.

The Kwanitekw roared, and the white, churning froth through the granite pass at the Ktsi Pôntekw was breathtaking, even for the seasoned Wawanolewat. It was too early for *mskwamagwok,* but they'd likely eat the sacred fish again in a few weeks. He led the group past the Ktsi Mskodak with their towering *koasak abaziak*, and his eyes roamed the hills just beyond where the former home of Zwame and Bilinto lay, and the large stone chambers. He reached the Wantatstekw, crossed its mouth completely concealed in *bakwaaskwol*, and headed over the hill through the trees, down toward Sokwakik.

But as he came to the crest of the ridge, his alarm mounted. There in the valley below a large group of colonists moved about, clearing and chopping on the meadow just by the carving of Pmola—only a league downriver from the mouth of Wantatstekw. Wawanolewat gave orders quickly.

"Tie and gag the prisoners—you four, spread out to see what the soldiers are doing. Don't be seen." For a few hours he and the four men studied the soldiers, looking closely at their work. A group of fifteen tents stood, no building as yet—but clearly they were preparing for one, with a massive pile of logs developing in the midst of a large, clear area of at least three acres. Easily fifty men stood working, and they carried arms and plenty of tools. They had apparently come up river in large canoes, fighting against the current. A number of them had native faces—a few Kanienkehaga, and it looked like two Mohican refugees from the great Mahiganek valley. Wawanolewat frowned. They should not be fighting Alnôbak and Pocumtuck peoples. Maybe they had no other choice. At closer observation, they were seen to wear gold and red emblems. Could they be designed to distinguish "friendly" natives in the heat of battle? That was well, then—they would also serve as targets for the arrows of his raiding party.

Under Wawanolewat, the group remained patient. They headed toward the west for a day, climbing into the hills toward the late-day sun; then they turned south toward Woronoco—a daring stroke, but close to Wawanolewat's heart. They stayed a fortnight at the mountain, looking out over the lowlands to the south, Pocumtuck land. Traveling southeast, they were pleased to find mostly unbroken woods all the way into the Westfield area. Late one evening, well into the night, the group gathered on the dramatic banks of the Woronoke, just above the English settlement. A three-quarter moon lit the forest floor, and they could easily see features of the land, washed in pale white.

Wawanolewat sat silent, meditating, and men dropped off for a nap. He awoke them well before dawn. As a unit, they stole down to a farm; then they split, one to set the barn afire, and the other to kill men running out of the house. They were successful on both counts—two men, one older, one younger, ran out with muskets—Wawanolewat and Malalemet stood at the ready. They attacked from either side, right by the door, in quick succession. Both men were quickly dispatched, and no more came out. The fire roared up in the hayloft as the arsonists ran straight back into the woods, due north. The party sent from Westfield to chase them fell way behind, and didn't have a chance.

Two days later the warriors spied a group of five men working in a meadow near Hatfield, and fell upon them, killing them all. From a hill two leagues to the north and west a few hours later, Wawanolewat used a spyglass he had recently obtained from Signeur de Niverville in Chambly to observe a group of soldiers headed north, along the banks of the Kwanitekw, chasing them in the wrong direction. He liked this new toy very much, and he used it often. Some things the Europeans made were really wonderful.

The swift, deadly phalanx of phantoms struck again in

Deerfield, and again in Northfield, and the men began to keep scalps at their belt in case bounties were offered in Canada. Through the territory, it seemed the warriors had no trouble striking and eluding chase at will—and it was their will, to wage destruction and terror. After all, the Pocumtuck homelands were now held hostage, systematically destroyed through the horrible "sale" of "property," leading to leveled forests, ugly, muddy cattle pasture, and huge fields of *skamonal* or *malomenal* with no sustenance—no fish, no beans, no ash to replenish the soil. Wanton destruction of the *wôbimiziak*—of all trees, really. No meadow and forest edge for game to grow in. Human waste dumped right into the streams. Dams on the smaller rivers, denying oceangoing fish the right to reproduce in their primordial springs. And now the first fort stood in Western Alnôbak territory—a British blockhouse in the dawnlands. Evil and evil. A canker on the land.

Nestled in a swampy hollow along the Kwanitekw one morning above Deerfield, Wawanolewat heard horses coming from the north. He bid the men lay low, and ran with three warriors up onto a small outcropping above the wide path the British used along the river. Three men came riding down on horseback, and they were snared like pheasants. Four native men jumped down onto the path in front of the horses, which reared even as eight more attacked from behind. The three riders and two horses were soon killed; one horse ran off, back up the path the way it had come. A few men began to scalp; as the party lingered on the path, a much larger group of soldiers came riding hard, from the north. Wawanolewat called a quick retreat, but the leaders were able to shoot three men, who nevertheless managed to run up the hill with some help into the deeper woods and swamp, where the horses couldn't follow. They kept on until they felt safe enough to stop. One Mazipskoi died along the way, and he had been quickly tucked under some tree branches. Another passed on when they halted, and was lain in a shallow grave. A third had an arm in a sling, a cloth tied tightly around a bleeding patch on his upper arm. Wawanolewat brooded, replaying the scene in his mind as a series of images ending with the faces of his men. *That beautiful horse gave us away.*

A week later, after traveling northwest and then northeast,

the raiding party again observed the blockhouse high up the Kwanitekw, below the mouth of Wantatstekw. Having taken careful notice of the men's activities, the raiding party stole to the north, took the canoes they had hidden, and paddled swiftly upriver and out of sight.

"Good thing we didn't stow these below the fort." Malalemet stated the obvious.

They made good time back up the Mkazawitekw and over the mountains, down Onegígwizibó and down the great Bitawbákw, past Odhihôzo. A few days later, in Chambly, they discussed the new fortification on the Kwanitekw with other sachems and signeur Monsieur de Niverville.

Anger at the British atrocity at Norridgewock still hung in the air. A few braves recounted the nasty massacre, though everyone knew the story. Father Rale, who had cared enough about Abenaki people to create a dictionary of the language, had been killed and mutilated, while soldiers slaughtered villagers mercilessly. All they could find.

The company listened to the men's account, silent. Wawanolewat's heart sought retribution for the invasion of the dawnlands. His voice rose clear. "I'll take another dive into their western nest. I'll bite their throat and rip out their heart with my talons. But I'll need fifty men or more." Various warriors agreed to join him.

In addition to ten or fifteen regular Pocumtuck and Sokwakiak companions, a large group of nearly thirty Mazipskoik signed on—powerful, proud, hardened warriors, angry at the idea of British in the dawnland. Other Pocumtuck and Mohican refugees from Schaghticoke had arrived, tired of living with policies of the Albany commissioners, and nine joined Wawanolewat's forces. One vocal member of their party, Schaschanaemp, pledged the Schaghticokes "will further kill and ravage the Massachussetts settlements to the best of our ability." Niverville dispatched five Frenchmen to accompany the group—a corporal and four cadets.

About seventy dawnlanders and the five bluebacked soldiers gathered a week later in the sunlight of Mazipskoik, on the marshes of the great lake. They rowed bateaux to Pointe a la

Chevalure, and crossed over the southern mountains toward tall Manicknung, and the river Wantatstekw. They camped comfortably at a bend in the river ten leagues north of the their target. Scouts were set up, and the men fished and hunted, and gathered their strength. Leaving some strips of meat at the camp to dry, they traveled down the rocky cleft of the river to the place of engagement. Wawanolewat knew the route well, as did many of them, and stealthily they came along the ridge to the south of the marshes at the mouth of Wantatstekw. Soon they were in a stand of *koasak* on the hilltop overlooking the bare clearing, with its large, square fort of light, newly cut and shaved logs, sides flattened by the adze. People moved like carpenter ants, in and out the entrance. The band of warriors watched silently, waiting unseen until dusk, when they followed shadows down the hillside to the fort. A small cannon was mounted on the northwest tower.

Wawanolewat ordered fifteen men to flank the fort on the right, and set a detachment of ten of the fastest and strongest to run and take the entryway if they could, while the French and a few dawnlanders with muskets attempted to sharpshoot the windows. As they charged, a cry went up from the fort, and sharp cracks and smoke of musketfire leapt from small, shuttered windows in the tower. With a blow across the jaw from a hatchet, a Mazipskoi Alôba named Adesh took out the guard by the front gate, and a group of five men threw themselves against the door just as it was thrown shut and held by a similar number of men on the other side. Fierce grunts were heard, and the latch clicked into place. The attackers were shut out. They fell back to the edge of forest, just out of easy musket range. As Adesh came running up, Wawanolewat kindled a large fire, and directed men to lay branches at the base of the palisades. Adesh grabbed an armful of wood, ran a zigzag pattern to the wall of the fort, and threw his sticks onto a growing pile. When he got back to the fire he said to Wawanolewat, "I'm going to light it!"

"Go, my brother!" came the reply.

The first cannon report echoed strong across the valley; the ball bounced at the edge of the clearing and crashed harmlessly into the trees, missing everyone. Adesh swept up a blazing hemlock branch and ran straight through the open space, whooping loudly. Musketfire sounded, and a ball whistled past his head, but he remained unmoved. The dry sticks and straw blazed up like hungry elementals in a fiery feast, licking the walls with a bright array of yellow, orange, and black tongues.

Calls from the inside led to a few buckets of water thrown over the walls, to little avail. The wall burned quite a bit before it blackened and died. It remained standing, not much damaged. The raiders watched from the woods, mostly unseen until late in the evening. The cannon did not fire again, no soldiers came from the fort, and Wawanolewat wondered if ammunition stores were low, and if they had a well inside the fort. They must, he thought. The site lay close to the river, and they must be able to get water from the southeast side. He set two warriors to cross just upriver and watch the fort from the south side. Two hours later, they reported back that there had been no activity. Tired of waiting, the entire group retreated due west under cover of night, along a broad brook south of Wantatstekw into some low hills, which the Sokwakiak called Wantastegok. They made a hasty camp some five leagues from the fort, nursed some burns and wounds, and posted watch.

Up on the hill overlooking the camp the following morning, Wawanolewat found a French cadet on watch, carving 1723 into a stone. The old man smiled, reminded of the petroglyphs at the Ktsi Pôntekw just upriver. He said, "I am glad you leave your mark on these hills—your people have been our friends, and we fight together as brothers."

The cadet introduced himself as Jean Baptiste, and shook Wawanolewat's hand. "I am proud to have kind words from such a renowned warrior." I have heard you have many names; here, the British know you as Grey Lock, and your infamy is unsurpassed; your peoples know you as Wawanolewat, or Wawanolewat, as you are so elusive, striking the British, and disappearing like a phantom; up at Chambly, you use a proper nom Française, do you not? Pierre Jean?

"Yes—you've heard true. In fact, many call me Pierre Jean dit la Tête Blanche, because of my hair. Your name, too, is impressive—I like the sound of it. Perhaps I will name a child after you someday."

"You honor me too greatly, sir."

"Not at all. Have you seen signs of the British this day?"

"Nothing—but I think they will come out today in as much force as they can, to engage us near the fort if they can find us. We could try to ambush the detachment."

"I'll send out scouting parties to locate any roving group of soldiers. We'll track and take them unawares."

He sent out three groups of three swift men—to the north, northeast, and to the east. He expected the northeast pair to find a battalion, and the colonists did not disappoint him. Wandering south along the mouth of Wantatstekw, a string of twenty green-coated soldiers marched in a slow and wary line with dawnland scouts at their head and tail. Wawanolewat silently spread his warriors along the ridge above them, with the Mazipskoiak en masse on a small hill, looking down the steepest, fastest slope down into the valley. At a drop of his hand they swept onto the soldiers, who scrambled for cover behind small boulders along the riverbank, or ran back toward the fort. In seconds the men were fighting in the shallows at the edge of the river, and the Alnôbak and other dawnlanders lost only three, while they killed ten and chased the others to the clearing north of the fort. Cannon fire boomed and smashed into the earth not far away, giving them a moment's pause. The door was opened to admit the British soldiers and the foremost scout. Before they made it in, the attackers overtook three more men and dropped them to the earth—two heads stoven by Adesh's club; one took a hatchet in the back, and soon bled out through his jugular. Stopping at the wall, the efficient detachment turned and sprinted back to safety at the edge of the large clearing, and rejoined their war party.

"Three more, Wawanolewat."

"Excellent. We had them completely by surprise. Now they won't go out so readily—I bet they don't even leave the fort to-morrow. We'll watch from right here." The raiding party set up camp right in the rolling hills just to the north of the fort, lit fires and whooped through the night. They sent fire arrows into the fort at times, and showed their fearlessness and scorn by running through the open meadows around the fort carrying burning branches, yelling taunts and obscenities. As expected, the colonists in the fort took a defensive position. Though they fired occasionally at the dawnlanders who entered the clearing that night, and the following day, the doors remained closed, and the colonists walled in. Wawanolewat estimated reinforcements would come within a day, if there were any soldiers to be had at Northfield, or two days if they had to come from Deerfield or Hadley. He did not doubt a message had somehow travelled downriver early in the first morning of the siege.

Wawanolewat broke his battalion into three groups. Jean Baptiste and the other soldiers headed back toward Pointe a la Chevalure with a few wounded dawnlanders. Adesh and the Mazipskoik headed southwest, charged with raiding any settlements they could find in the border town of Colraine, Northfield, or along the road to Fort Wilderness, near Stockbridge. Wawanolewat himself led eleven Sokwakiak and Pocumtuck due east, across the river and up the Ashuelot, then turning south toward the beaver's tail again to strike British settlements east of the Kwanitekw. They were so helpless; terrorizing these people seemed easy, like taking *temakwak* from their lodges in midwinter. At first snowfall, the party headed home to Mazipskoik. In the spring, Wawanolewat thought, he would head to Schaghticoke and see if any of his people residing there still carried strength in their hearts, and in their clubs.

1733

The new decade brought relative quiet, but political tension remained as British and French jockeyed for the loyalty of various native bands. The British maneuvers were in vain; no way would the large majority of Western Alnôbak and Pocumtucks ever join any military alliance with the English king. Somehow the eastern Abenakis came to terms with the British colonists in Msajosek, the hilly, former Pocumtuck lands—probably because they were terrified, following the massacres of the previous decade, believing they had no choice; over in New York, most of the Hodinohso:ni nation continued a loose alliance with the British in the area of Albany and Renssalearwyck, anyway. While the peace lasted, fur business boomed in the great triangle trade of mercantilism.

A merchant whom all the natives liked, a Dutchman named John Henry Lydius, set up shop in the Great Crossing Place between the Muheannaheanock or North River (which some now called the Hudson) and Pointe a la Chevalure, which the British called Crown Point. Lydius had been exiled by the French, but he was a good trader, and he even spent time educating some of the Schaghticokes—teaching them to read English, learning Psalms from the King James Bible.

A new French fort had been erected at Crown Point, called Fort St. Frederic, and the monsignor maintained a respectable business in baptism, marriage, and funerals.

Closer to home in Mazipskoik, the smallpox again reared its head, and many people had moved to Odanak—when things became bad there, some even retreated to Acadia. Populations remained about the same, though. The death toll was high, but it seemed River Indians disenchanted with years of self-serving Albany treaties continually arrived from Schaghticoke and other refugee centers, As a result, the cultural identities were constantly changing, and Wôbanaki gradually became the mother tongue of a broad diaspora at Mazipskoiodanak.

Atahla was gone, lost to typhoid. Wawanolewat continued to live in his little village with a new wife, named Helene. A Mazipskoik, she had dark, straight hair and dark eyes, and at forty-three years, she was considerably younger than her new husband. But Wawanolewat, despite his grey and white hair, continued to seem limber and ageless, though it was rumored he was close to seventy-five years old! The two of them even had a child together—young Marie-Charlotte, not more than a year old—and now, Helene was looking (and acting) pregnant again. Wawanolowet's son Noluwey, now nineteen, moved out of the house, north to Trois Rivieres.

Zwame noted all these things with interest as she went about her work, making baskets in the mornings, and in the afternoons taking on a variety of domestic tasks. She had not been needed up at Chambly since the war's end, and she and Bilinto had lived relatively happily despite the ravages of disease in the greater community, and the ongoing war that the dawnland peoples had remained engaged in through most of the 1720s. She was now fifty, and silver crept into her blonde hair, lending her a certain dignity, as if her status as Wawanolewat's daughter were not enough. Men treated her with great respect—along with Helene, she ranked among the most powerful women in her community. At times she reflected how powerless and relatively unimportant she would be in her original society, had she remained the daughter of John and Abigail Sackett. Doubtless she would have married an Englishman, lived in a cramped cabin with many children and days of hard labor; she'd have spent endless hours worshiping an unfriendly God, repenting the 'horrible sins' she had committed by thinking about another man, or just by wishing she were somewhere else! How lucky she was, to have been captured and spared such dark drudgery. Still, she planned a trip south again within the next few weeks, to see if her father still lived—to have one last visit, a final chance to say goodbye.

Namito had become a full-grown man, thirty years of age, and everyone but his close relatives called him 'Saksis,' or "Sachette." His family sentiments and the hostility of the Mazipskoiak toward the English had long ago drawn him in—he fought with Wawanolewat in his later raids, in 1726 and 27, and since then had spent much time up at Chambly receiving semi-formal military training, always anticipating an end to the cold war which had lasted nearly twenty years between the French and English, since the Treaty of Utrecht.

Young Saksis received his best training on raids with Wawanolewat and other warlike Mazipskoiak during the 1720s. Now, partly to get away from disease in the village center, a Mazipskoiak named Philip de Chaudelait gathered a small group of fifteen men from the Richelieu valley to trap and train in the wooded Abenaki homelands between Bitawbákw and the Kwanitekw—a wild land of low hills, *bôbenodagwezak* and hardwood forests, *temakwak* lodges and wetlands—still full of game, unlike so many of the settled valleys now—*mozak* and *wôboz* wandered there, plenty of *nolkak* and *awasosak, môlsemak,* endless waterfowl. Drawn by the desire to travel, hunt, and to strengthen the family economy, Saksis joined them. There were good monies to be made from trapping.

The young man quickly learned a variety of methods—snares, deadfalls, and lures. The natives hated the biting traps of the Frenchmen, which often damaged the fur and caused great pain to the animals; with the pride of artists, the Wôbanakiak preferred to manage in their own way. Sackett's particular methods were very traditional, and very direct. He enjoyed the quiet, and preferred to hunt alone.

By day he wandered through seemingly endless fields of the white, stripped logs and branches which indicated *temakwak* wetland. If *wôbozak, mozak,* or small herd *nolkak* presented, he would stalk the animals, keeping just out of sight, downwind, trying to circle round until he was ahead of their path. Then he'd wait for them to come up on him, and offer an easy shot—his crossbow, purchased in Montreal for eighty livres, sang powerful and true.

Maybe four out of ten large animals fell to him, if he were able to flank them in this way. The most exciting hunting, though, came at dusk.

Each evening as the daylight waned, he lurked silently, stealthily at the edge of a shallow pool, near a fertile field of *temakwak* lodge. He carefully selected each pool specifically for its depth, width, and narrow inlet. The animals were completely predictable. At dawn, and again at dusk, after the sun dipped below the western horizon, the dark shapes broke the surface of the water sending spreading V's rippling toward the shore. Their powerful tails swishing firmly through the water, the animals made busy, gathering wood, food, floating and moving large logs toward the lodge.

Saksis waited until three or more hove into short range, near to his hiding place, well within the confines of the pool. Moving like flashing water, brandishing a club, he darted around the edge of the pool to the inlet, where he sprang upon the closest animal and bashed it severely on the head. The others swam quickly away toward the opposite shore of the small pool, but they could never escape. Leaping through the water like a *nolka*, he fell upon them and dispatched them easily. Then, using his large steel knife, he quickly gutted them.

He returned to camp every evening with three to six skins. Most others hunted in this way; few used traps on a regular basis, though they all knew how to make them. Each evening, forty or more new skins were cleaned, scraped, dipped in tannic solutions made from boiling *alnizediak* bark, or hollowing *mekwisagezok* stumps and filling them with water. In the morning, he hung the skins to dry, then sent them with a pair of hunters back to their village, or the nearest trading post, whichever was closer.

Sometimes they'd range south to Fort Dummer, where a worldly Brit named Joseph Kellogg held court as the new truckmaster. Kellogg traveled to Canada after his capture at Deerfield at age twelve—he numbered among the children who marched north under Rouville, Wawanolewat, and the others, and he had lived at Chambly for several years, learning French, Alnôbak, and Kahnawake Kanienkehaga. His linguistic skills proved invaluable to the British, and they encouraged him to set up shop at the blockhouse on the Connecticut. He quickly developed a busy trading post where he promised cheap goods for sale to all comers. A minister named Ebenezer Hinsdale arrived as well, and began a regular effort at teaching visiting dawnlanders the Protestant path. One good thing about Dummer was, there wasn't as much alcohol as they found in New York. Rum and whiskey made men feel powerful, but the long-term results were always depressing. He had a simple rule, that Wawanolewat followed before him—no drinking on the trail, or while raiding. For stealth, they needed judgment, and to work as a team there could be no violent aggression among them. Alcohol was a serious liability.

If Saksis' group were further west, they'd trade at Fort St. Frederic, or, best of all, John Henry Lydius' camp. Lydius generally offered better prices than any of the French or English traders. Apparently demand was high in Albany and parts south, and Lydius did quite well. The natives guessed his competitive pricing was the reason he'd been exiled, and frequently asked authorities at forts along Bitawbákw—known to the French and English now as "Champlain"—if he could return. The Kahnawake encouraged the British to allow him to build a fort on the Onegígwizibó, across from Fort St. Frederic, hoping to develop price wars between British and French. The Kahnawake even alleged that Lydius had bought land in that area, but no one could produce legal documents to support this claim. In the end, these native hopes were never realized, but with a little extra travel they could reach him along the portage trail to the Mahiganek, and trade with him there. Evenings at the Dutchman's camp were fun, and could be raucous.

Saksis roamed with his band of skinners and traders, buying and selling, when they weren't harvesting *temakwak* fields. He and his group became known at many posts, though none of the colonial British realized he was grandson of Wawanolewat. One time at Fort Dummer, speaking with Kellogg and a Schaghticoke Mohican named Kakadolôkok, he explained that he was born and lived much of his childhood just upriver, by the Ktsi Mskodak. Kellogg asked, "Exactly where?"

But Saksis would not reveal the specific location of the stone chambers where his family resided, and still retained stores of food in time of need, during raids which might develop in the years ahead. Instead he replied vaguely, "Along the stream there, that comes in just below the Meadow where the old maples are." Saksis knew Kellogg had his particular motives. A lot of money could be made from land and resources. These were the front lines of power, in the peaceful times.

"If your family lived there, and your father is truly Sokwaki, then you can sell to us. Governor Belcher would give you fifty pounds sterling for the portion of land known as the Ktsi Mskodak. You'd only need one or two other Wôbanaki signatures to certify your ownership, and make it all legal."

"I'd never sell to British. Never, as long as I draw breath and the Alnôbak hold any power in the dawnlands. You have as much chance of selling to my family as shooting salmon in the forest." He looked Kellogg directly in the eye. Don't try to buy the land north of here. You'll bring back enemies you wish you never had. Your worst enemies will be back here to see you. Listen, we'll trade with you. We'll deal in fur and guns and hatchets. But watch you don't get to wanting the land."

"I'm just the middle man. There will always be someone to replace me, and there will always be colonists wanting land." Kellogg turned up his palms, and shrugged.

"I pray to God, there will always be first peoples to stop you."

Still, Kellogg remained hopeful. Some people, traveling upriver from the fort, came to know the western stream below the Meadow as "Sackett's brook." But, Kellogg knew, many had their eyes on that land. And he wouldn't deny them the opportunity.

$$\approx \bigcirc \approx$$

While the peace still lingered, Zwame headed south to see her blood relatives. She herself was now over fifty, and if he lived, her father would be close to ninety. Gihla joined her, and after a hard paddle down the choppy Bitáwbakw, they followed well-beaten trails from Onegígwizibó to the Kwanitekw, where they took the family canoe (so often used for Wawanolewat's raids) down to Springfield, and then up the Woronoke to Westfield. It no longer seemed like natural, original land, and she hardly felt it merited the old names—it had transformed so completely. Doubtless Wawanolewat would have a different opinion.

This time, Gihla waited at the edge of the property, while Zwame trudged along the rutted wagon trail toward the homestead. At her family home she found her brother John in his seventies, living with his wife Mahitable and son Daniel. Her father had passed away fourteen years before. Her nephew and his stepmother looked on Zwame with the distrustful eyes of strangers regarding an 'other' culture, but her brother seemed surprisingly warm. He invited Zwame in, and the two sat down facing one another on wooden chairs in John's parlor, which now had a wooden floor, a shallow hearth, and a round, coiled carpet. John took his time with each sentence, and seemed headed for a long heart-to-heart.

"Bethie! Bless your soul. I can't believe I really have the chance to see you one more time, after all these years. It's like my Christmas dreams come true. It was horrible when they took you, girl. They burned our barn. They killed children—we thought they killed you. Were you mad at us when we didn't find you? I have had so many questions all these years." Apparently he needed to go through the explanations all over again, as if Zwame had never visited them, twenty years before. Feeling safer now, Zwame asked if she could invite Gihla to join them, which she did.

Then she continued, thoughtfully. "No, the people were good to me. I was young. I thought of you and missed you, but I felt happy with them, too. I got to know them after a few weeks. They were warmer than our home was—what I remember of our traditions. Our parents didn't hold us much or smile a lot, and it was hard to do the right thing—I mean I remember a lot of criticism, a negative feeling."

"Well, that may be true. I was never able to imagine what an Indian home is like for the children, though I often tried after you were taken away. You say the people were friendly?" Her brother seemed skeptical.

"Yes, we smile much more than you might guess. Our friends and family took part in games, contests, and all kinds of other things. They had time to spend with me, and I had freedom to roam as I liked. I'd never had anything like that before."

"Well, I guess not. Your new family treated you well, even when you were little?"

"Yes. All my life. There are so many wonderful stories among my people. There is no way to compare them with the scary stories of God I knew as a child. I was lucky to escape your people. I'm sorry to say it, but it's true."

"Well, I never heard such a surprising story. I'm sorry, I can't just believe that. While you were there in Canada, did you become Catholic?" His eyes flashed for a moment. "Did the Papists get their claws into you?"

Zwame smiled patiently. "Yes, I did spend a good deal of time with Catholics, and one priest in particular has taken an interest in my family. My Woronoke parents, born on this land before our parents even moved here, were baptized last year—they're starting to hold the Jesuit God in the same reverence as some of our most powerful gods. Personally, I don't have any interest in the Catholic God, or your Protestant God. I love the old stories, the dawnland spirits that inhabit this land, and my only creator is Ktsi Niwaskw. My memories of your God, from my childhood, leave a bad taste."

John Sackett's eyes hardened as she spoke, then softened again. "Girl, you blaspheme—but I love you still, and your mother loved you dearly. You are my own sister. Your name has changed, but you'll carry my love, and your mother's love, to your grave. As this may be the last I see of you, I give you my blessing. I give you my love." A tear rolled down his wrinkled cheek, and Zwame was moved in her heart. She embraced the old man, and they held each other quietly, alone in a small room in the cabin, while sounds of chopping came in from the yard. Gihla watched in silence. Finally, the siblings parted.

Back in Westfield, the elderly John Sackett felt redeemed, having regained something important he'd lost, long before. Along the route home, Zwame also felt peace in her heart, as if that chapter were finally settled. Sewing in the canoe, her thoughts turned to troubled times, with clearer lines of hatred—reliving memories from when she was just a young mother, and Wawanolewat's leadership waxed strong.

1738

A few years later, the family rocked unpredictably, slipping from side to side, with nothing firm beneath them. They tried to hold fast to their seats.

"Where away?"

"Two points off starboard."

"Make for the flat rock point."

Namito brought the bow up through the eye of the wind, bringing the fifteen-foot wooden whaleboat about on a close-hauled path to hail another vessel headed south. A dramatic, flat outcropping loomed way ahead. A telltale at the top of the mast showed a southeasterly wind, gusty. They had to fight to stay up, but they moved quickly, almost slapping across Bitáwbakw.

Wawanolewat, nearly eighty, set the small, lateen-rigged sail and leaned on the outboard gunwale, riding the wind and the waves. His wife Helene huddled amidships with their daughter Marie Charlotte, who'd just been baptized at Fort St. Frederic. Their second child, a boy, had died in childbirth.

The occupants of the other, similar boat hove into view. Well-made deerskin pants and shirts, full, dark hair in ponytails. Wawanolewat called out to his crew, "Mohican!"

The other boat passed aft, and Namito hailed them. "Headed to Schaghticoke?"

"Stockbridge!"

"Why in the hell you want to live in that British village?" Wawanolewat wanted to know. "It's completely muddy!"

"They take care of us. We get blankets, food, liquor. It's a good life!" They had to shout to be heard.

Namito called loudly, "No! Come north, where the Wôbanakiak are strong!" They merely shrugged and smiled, as they pulled quickly out of earshot.

Wawanolewat/Greylock muttered loudly, "Fools. They are pursued by smoke." Namito nodded.

They rounded two more points of land, and three hours later passed Odzihozo, who sat in the lake like a lord protector. They rounded up with a dramatic jibe in the easterly wind, right in front of the Alnôbak god, to scatter some tobacco on the water as they passed. Another couple of tacks, and an hour later they scraped up on the eastern shore, unstepping the mast, and pulling the whaleboat into the usual hiding spot. They headed into low pine and hemlock forest, up a winding path into the hills, and came out on the main path to Wawanolewat's family compound.

At home, Zwame greeted them with plenty of hot *skamonal* pone and *bebonkiimadeqwasal* stew. Namito laughed with his mother, and his grandfather settled into his comfortable bunk, watching the fire, features chiseled and experience lining his face. More than ever before, he resembled a powerful wizard.

Between soft *awasosok* skins, Gihla slept. She felt comfortable in her grandfather's secure retreat, the palisade which had become like a hometown to her over the past two decades. This was ancient Alnôbak land, home of the Mazipskoik, long a refuge of troubled indigenous peoples from the south, east, and west. She went to bed thinking of all the safe people around Wawanolewat's village, and in the lowlands of Mazipskoik, at the entrance to the Richelieu.

Her sleepings, as it turned out, were once again less than comforting; the hot midsummer night dragged on, sweaty and unsettling. She managed some astral travel, slipping in and out of spiritual realms; she could feel all the land surrounding Bitáwbakw and the Kwanitekw under threat of invasion. She saw waves of colonists coming, hundreds of thousands. She fought against them, but they overtook her like a sandstorm. They pulled Mazipskoiak leaders into their courts and made them beg for their homelands. They called the Alnôbak liars, and took the land away. They said it was Hodinohso:ni land. Kanienkehagaki land. Used to bad dreams, she made it through, but she remembered upon awakening, and the images troubled her.

Gihla explained her dream to her mother and brother, in the morning, and Namito became troubled. He felt an impulse to leave, to visit the southern homelands.

Wawanolewat stood in the doorway as Namito pulled his *skamon* sack, weapons, and a few other items together.

"You need to see something?"

Namito replied, "Yes, grandfather. I think they are coming into our lands more and more. Gihla feels it in her dreams. I want to know what the situation is."

"I'm glad you're going. We need to know what passes with them."

Wizwame, grinding *skamonal*, said, "You will find things you don't like. But remember, they are different from you. Destroying the land makes them feel safe."

"It makes me feel unsafe."

"It makes all of us unsafe." Gihla stated the obvious.

Namito spoke at last. "I will see what I will see." He ran off, up the hill, toward the mountains.

Namito cut straight across the tallest ridge, and descended into the Koasek valley. The tall *koasak* of the intervals greeted him, majestic and friendly. People came out to say hello.

Arriving in the village he saw a Sokwaki he knew named Pinawans, as well as many others among the friendly Koasiaks. They smiled and waved. As Bilinto's son, Namito was family. He walked the village paths. People seemed happy, scraping skins, sewing, weaving, keeping trade going. Maize grew along the riverbank,

"What news, Pinawans?" Namito's old friend sat sharpening knives by the edge of a meadow. Mskwamagok fillets hung in rows, drying in the summer sun.

"Ho, Sackett! Well met on a beautiful morning. You traveling southward, or staying for a season?"

"Can't. Looking at the homeland, south. Just taking a look."

"Well, can't say as you'll like what you see. Bostoniak moving in, wanting wood. Nechehoosqua, Massequnt's wife—Sokwaki, you know her, from over to Schaghticoke? Leased a patch of land north of Fort Dummer. I let her—don't know what I was thinking. She was on hard times, and I didn't know the part they was talking about until after. I signed on it, but then I tried to get them to take it off the papers. They wouldn't let me do it."

"Where? Not the Ktsi Mskodak! The old forest?"

"Afraid so. Nothing to be done now. Lotta trees missing. I am very sorry. I know Bilinto brought you up there."

"*Tabarnacula*! I'll head straight off tomorrow. Damn your eyes, Pinawans."

Namito headed south in a small canoe the next morning, with a decent store of *skamonal*. *Temakwak* broke the early morning water, and appeared again close to evening. He saw a number of *moskwak* as well. He enjoyed the acrobatic, dipping *benegôkihlasizak*, and dropped a line in close to dinner, bringing up *môlaziganak*. Dinner gave itself to him readily, easy and flavorful, with crackling fish skin, tender meat, and plenty of *winozak* and *sôsowipogwagak*. He slept on a soft, *asakwamal* bank, with a blanket warding off *begwes*.

The next day saw more glorious travel down the river valley, rich in wildlife. In the evening, he slept in a dry nook of carved stone, the Kwanitekw raging through the granite passage of the Ktsi Pôntekw, only a short distance away. He portaged his craft to the lower river, and paddled off. In the late morning his old familial homeland, the Ktsi Mskodak, came into view.

It was near to decimated. Leveled. Scarred and ugly.

Stumps of more than six feet diameter ranged all around. The forest floor was strewn with pine branches, all dead and brown.

Forest girded the clearcut area, some tall trees, some younger, but none of it had any thick, healthy meadow's edge of tall bushes and saplings. Scraggly bushes and smaller *koasak* poked up through the layers of dead branches.

Namito, horrorstruck, nevertheless had a sense of guilty déjà vu. He had known this was happening. He'd been able to feel it. But he was too late to defend it. He felt angry, hated the colonists for destroying this ancient, sacred place. He hated their careless attitude, how they seemed to enjoy laying things to waste. His people were not given to quick anger, but it consumed him now with a cold, durable flame.

He built a fire, and chanted into the evening, along with the crackling, broken branches. He ground the blackened ash, pulverized berries, and painted his face. In the morning, he left a pile of branches burning, knowing it would burn up a huge lot in a massive brush fire. *Let the meadow be cleansed, at least a little, by fire. The colonists will try to move north. Let them come. I will kill them, personally. We will kill them, and burn their houses. They will have to leave.*

He moved out in to the river. Pieces of bark lined the riverbank, especially on the western bank. One large log lay wedged between the shore and a rocky island not far away, trapped by the current. Namito saw a crown with 1735 just below, branded into its massive base. *So these were the king's men. They rape our woods for the British navy.* Namito had seen large, seagoing boats on the Ktsitekw, and he knew of the British dominance on the water. He thought of the shipbuilding industries developing on the Massachusetts coast, and of leveled forests across the eastern woodlands, cleared for ships, houses, fires, farmland. He stomach lurched, and he vomited. How could they do this without asking his family? *This is Sacketts brook!*

He followed the sickly river, littered with branches, foam and sawdust, to Fort Dummer.

Within the walls of the fort, Kellogg had nothing useful to say. "She sold it. A lot of Sokwakiak signed the deed. Nechehoosequa daughter of Conkesemah, wife of Auma Sacooaneh, Sokwakiak Indians of Schatighcoke. Now the land belongs to the crown of England. It's not just some colonist what bought that land."

"It wasn't hers to sell. That document was a lease only. Shared use. Not a sale! You know that as my family's brook, just below it. You know my father is Sokwaki. How could you 'sell' that?"

"Listen. I didn't sign the paper." Passing the baton of blame. "It was the woman who wanted the money, and Governor Belcher needed the trees."

"I think you'll be sorry sometime. I'm not saying I'm about to do anything. But you will put fire in dawnland hearts, with destroying that forest. Those pines were put there by our Creator. He said it—he made them. He wanted it that way. It is not for you to change. I feel the fire. Hot."

"It is good wood. The best. It will grow back."

"Not likely. Not in your grandchildren's lifetime. You seen any British colonies, ever? How many four hundred year old trees you see?"

Kellogg smiled. "I can't argue. You're right. You know, I never thought about it that way."

Fire burned in Namito's eye. "Think about it now." He left. He headed north, on the river. At Wantatstegok, he gathered cattail tubers. Further up the Kwanitekw, he passed the meadow. He muttered quietly to himself.

"Idiots. I'll kill them all."

He decided to take the Black River, and cross the ridge to Otter Creek. As he hid the canoe carefully against a pair of small trees upstream, he noticed thinking with the British names for the first time. Sardonically, he reflected: Why not use the British names? What the hell did it matter now? Wouldn't it all be British in a matter of years? He knew how Wawanolewat would feel about this bit of reflection. *Okay, old one. No more British names.*

Namito had never yearned for war more than he did now. Not a war to defend the land. A war of retribution.

He could organize a group of killers like drawing wasps to honey, when it came to it. He would fight in the old way, with the new weapons. Even if he had British blood, he could not understand the reasoning behind the destruction of the majestic pine groves. No ships or cities merited their loss. No group of people could gain luxury and prominence from this act of destruction, without a strong guilt and evildoing. These were tainted actions. They would bring bad luck on everyone involved. The Spirit could not rest, now, until the Dawnland responded to this canker of humanity, this infestation, this mound of British termites. As he walked, he threw his tomahawk viciously into trees along the path.

His mind continued in this vein until he arrived at Fort St. Frederic. The birds sang and the mountain paths glowed in magical sunlight, but he had little joy in them. He traveled quickly, stopping only to replenish a couple of mountain stores along the way, in constant anticipation of his return trip.

1745

Nehemiah Howe had spent much of the early morning setting a back cut on one of the remaining, 150-plus foot white pine on the Great Meadows. His sharp axe bit easily through the seemingly endless white flesh. When he felt it was deep enough, he walked back to his small fort and called to Bill Phipps, across the field hoeing corn, to help fetch the saw.

Phipps met him at the house, and they carried the recently sharpened, two-handled saw together toward the tree. A catbird had been singing all morning near the tree, but it was quiet now. The late morning sun shone brightly in the clearing, and the men's feet were wet from dew, still filling the thick grass. The men placed the blade against the trunk, above and opposite Howe's cut, and had just begun the back-and-forth motions when Bill spoke up.

"I always remember my gloves after the first few passes. I'll be right back."

Howe grunted. He'd been wearing his all morning. He watched Bill trudge off across the expanse of meadow, with wildflowers, near a patch of dark, brown soil they'd been working. He turned back to look at the tree.

Phipps' voice rang out across the clearing. "Howe! Indians!"

When he turned, Phipps had grabbed a hoe and was sprinting for the fort, with two Alnôbak flying along behind him. They nearly reached him, and he turned and swung the hoe hard around, catching one in the side of the head, jerking the neck sickeningly. The man fell on the spot, and the other stepped back quickly while Phipps turned to run again. Right then, Bill caught a musket ball in his rib cage, and as he staggered, another entered his back. He fell, but he caught one of his attackers in the leg with the hoe on the way. The Indian kneeled over him, and turned toward Howe, who hid behind a tree.

Howe saw the man give his commander a look and a jerk of the head, which seemed to say *I'm hurt, and there's a man behind that tree.*

Saksis, now a full-grown warrior over forty, strode confidently toward Howe, who fell to the ground and raised his hands over his head in surrender. "Get up," Saksis commanded. "Walk." He pointed toward the fort. He went over to look at Michel Mantok, the Mazipskoiak who had fallen. Dead. François Lussier fared better; the man jammed the blade of the hoe up into his hamstring, but he could walk, and would heal. Saksis cleaned the bruised gash, dressed it, and handed him a good walking stick.

Four other Alnôbak joined them in the clearing, and twenty more waited by the fort. They set about destroying the stores, taking what they could easily carry, and hauling off the sacks of maize into the woods for storage. The few cattle grazing outside the fort, they slaughtered. Though they were used to seeing heifers up in Chambly and Montreal, they found these complacent animals strange—a symbol of the fenced-off style of property ownership the British had, for which they needed to clearcut large portions of land to be allowed to keep them. The warriors spread entrails around the clearing, enjoying Howe's grimace as they scooped out and flung the organs. There would be no mistaking their warlike intent. Maybe the next colonists to come along would think a while before setting their blades to the ancient trees of the great meadow. One of the braves, Konnegwak, said, "This'll make quite a dinner tonight."

They dragged carcasses to a nearby house. "Cut the meat from the bones. I'll put out our signals. The scouts will join us soon." While the men carried out Saksis' orders, spoken in Alnôbak, he cut off the head of Howe's axe and set it in the ground pointing north. They set out laden with beef, moving fairly slow, because of François.

Saksis tied Howe's hands, and bid him walk. Howe was pretty

new along the river, and didn't know him from his regular trading down at Fort Dummer in previous years. As he quickly trudged along the path, he questioned Saksis. " What leads you to this bloody display of power? I've been peaceful, respectful, quiet. What are your designs?"

Saksis looked him dead in the eye. "You are of the people who leveled this holy forest. Now, finally, war is declared. We are tired of your pushing north, your destruction of the old world. The trees on this meadow, cut by the King's men. The death of thousands of our relatives these past decades. And we are allied with France, who would war with you. We are ready and willing." He said it in cold blood, deadly serious. He had resisted sneering and sarcasm. Howe nodded, seeming to understand the stakes at last. He'd been a fool, to settle upriver.

They headed north. Wantatstekw seemed too dangerous, too close to the big Dummer blockhouse. They traveled a day up the Kwanitekw, headed for the Mkazawitekw river. Near to the Ktsi Pôntekw, the captive Howe started yelling, and banging a large stick against a nearby tree. Right at that moment a man from forward part of the line called the reason: "Two Englishmen on the river!" Howe had seen them. The two men, alarmed, paddled hard away from the group, to the other side of the river. The group loaded their arms quickly and fired—Saksis, with an amazing shot, put a ball in one man's neck, but the other got away. A small detachment swam across for the canoe. They scalped the dead man, whom Howe identified ruefully: "David Rugg, a man of my fort."

Just before the falls, they came to a small cabin they kept deep in a patch of conifers, pulled out a big cooking pot, and got the fires going. An hour later, some ways distant, branches broke and leaves rustled. Colonists? "Go!" Saksis spoke to a group of six men, and they ran off in chase. Half an hour later they returned, reporting they'd found the trail of a bear. The party relaxed. They walked on again, another mile upriver, and stopped for the night. That night they fattened up on beef from Howe's fort, and slept well on the forest floor. They agreed they would not need food for a day or two now.

The next morning they headed slowly up to Fort No. 4. Having stopped here on the way down, they knew the fort stood empty, and they'd spend the night there. In the morning, Saksis decided to leave a few souvenirs as a false trail for the soldiers who would surely be along soon. He said to Howe, "write your name on this bark—say also how many days we've traveled." Howe did as he was told, and Saksis nailed the bark to a tree at the mouth of a stream just north of the fort, on the east side of the river.

They crossed the river, headed a bit south, and turned west at the Mkazawitekw, following its winding path high into the mountains. Howe labored on, but didn't complain. He seemed thoughtful, and showed good manners, but he looked weak and hungry. At times, he uttered the Lord's Prayer, which Saksis had heard frequently in the trading posts, in the circles of worship the British were always pulling together. The words sounded powerful, and Howe seemed able to bear the journey well when he spoke them.

The narrow old Alnôbak path snaked further and further into the mountains. Saksis doubted the British knew this way at all. The stream finally flowed small, and they crested the divide, following the ridge a bit south; then they stopped at a small shelter Saksis and crew kept in a hollow, protected by a cliff to the southeast. They boiled up a big kettle of corn, salt, and cooked beef, which some of the men still carried wrapped in leaves. They had beer as well, which they had set to brew in jars, and they all enjoyed an excellent repast.

In the morning, feeling renewed, they headed west again at a better pace, to the river that would lead them to Bitawbákw and the Abenaki settlement by Pointe a la Chevalure. It took two days to accomplish this traverse. Saksis told Howe, "if you don't walk fast today, we'll kill you." Like generations of raiding Wôbanakiak before him, his philosophy was simple: walk, run, or die. For over a century, people of the eastern woodlands had found that approach a fairly effective inspiration for the soft Europeans, who could really cover a reasonable distance without complaining too much if motivated correctly. Besides, they needed hardening, and they had sins to atone for.

The day waxed, cool and refreshing, with a fine, soft breeze that remained steady as they wove through the rocky hills. Along the trail, Saksis observed Howe's discomfort in his hobnailed wood-and-hard-leather shoes, and gave him some moccasins instead. Howe put them on obediently, and gratitude showed immediately on his face. "Foolish shoes they wear," Saksis remarked to Konnegwak, who replied,

"Unbelievable. His feet must have huge blisters."

He added, "Our food is low. What say a group of us stop to hunt?"

"Sounds good. Plenty of game. Why don't you see who feels like going out?"

Konnegwak quickly had twelve men dispersing in different directions, and in three hours they returned with two *awasosak*, a young *nolka*, and four *nahamak*. They roasted and devoured these, and moved on. Again, they headed west, and soon were headed down the rushing Onegígwizibó. They made good time, spent one more night in the woods, and late the following morning, Howe was still doing well. Konnegwak encouraged him, saying half-mockingly, "You are a strong Englishman!" Howe managed a smile.

By mid-afternoon, the lake hove into view. At the water's edge five canoes waited, camouflaged in a hollow with some buried foodstuffs. Saksis took Rugg's scalp and put it up on a pole, to ward off British followers from Fort Wilderness, if they should push north. One of the men, a Kahnawake named Jean Jacques, painted it red with a leering face. "Looks suitably forbidding," he noted to Konnegwak, who smiled in agreement.

They piled in the canoes and paddled north, and after a couple of hours went ashore for supper and sleep. They untied Howe, and gave him some food. Then they rested, and in the morning it was only a few hours up to Pointe a la Chevalure. Before they arrived, a small group of their friends spotted them, and two of them waded excitedly out into the water to beach the canoe, and bring Howe ashore.

"Well done!" The newcomers eyed the prisoner with interest. Everyone felt lively, now war had been declared.

"This is the man from the Ktsi Mskodak? Did you wreck the fort properly, then?" They were abuzz with hopes that the British could be kept from the upper Kwanitekw.

Singing and dancing followed a few hours later, and they paraded Howe around the fire. Then they sat him down, and Saksis took off the moccasins and the buckles they used for restraint. The party traveled the rest of the way to the stone and lime fort, well populated with French and natives of all kinds. The small pack of men ran Howe up to the fort, and up the stairs into the captain's chamber. Saksis gave him a chair, and he sat by the fire awhile, while men outside discussed plans for the evening. Pealtomy and Amrusus, both garrisoned at Pointe a la Chevalure, knew Howe well, and went in to keep him company. Amrusus married a former Deerfield captive, who like Wizwame, was now one of them.

Evening wore on, and the mood became festive. "Got me a Puritan!" Konnegwak shouted. The men bantered about the victories they'd soon have over the Massachusetts colonists. Everyone naturally expected the prisoner would provide some entertainment. He had to perform, to bring them luck in battles ahead. His dancing would fertilize their designs. François, much better now, said, "What about it then? Let's make him dance." This suggestion met with wide acclaim. The men sat in a ring in the courtyard, and Pealtomy brought Howe down for a performance.

Pealtomy spoke to Howe. "I suggest you do what you're asked." The group appointed a man to teach Howe some Alnôbak, and the bearded man resisted a bit, pretending he was confused. Finally, he danced, and sang their song. The men laughed. It felt good to see at least one Englishman act the fool on purpose, instead of the usual blustering ignorance of their own idiocy; self-righteous and sure of their God's dominance, they did and said foolish things; they looked and acted like idiots unaware of themselves. This performance had more honesty, and proper reflection.

Saksis had seen many captives look considerably more foolish than this kind man, who'd offered to help around camp, now that he had rested a bit from the trek. They accepted his offer, and in a few days some began to like him. Still, he was headed up the lake, and before long Saksis sent him on his way with a contingent of Kahnawake headed for Montreal. "Take him to

Governor Vaudreille, and see him imprisoned."

"No problem." The men made to tie his hands.

"You don't need to tie this one. He'll go along without trouble."

The Kahnawake helped Howe into their bateaux and pushed off. Saksis and Howe watched one another for a few hundred meters. The distance grew, and finally he turned back up the trail into the woods.

≈≈○≈≈

None of the men were much inclined to head home, and as the grandson of Wawanolewat, they looked to Saksis as their leader. He responded to the apparent vacuum of their ambition.

"So what would you men have? Another trip down the Kwanitekw? Shall we bring death to a few English soldiers?"

The men took turns speaking. "We love to raid the villages."

"What are we here for? There is no more important work to accomplish."

"You are always successful, Saksis. We follow you willingly."

It quickly became clear everyone was thrilled to be back at war, and they were ready to travel south again. The opportunity to wage indiscriminate destruction on the settlements offered a welcome break from hunting and peaceful trade. There were many scores to settle. As Saksis' numbers quickly swelled again to twenty, he headed back up the river and over the divide, this time dropping further south along the ridge, until they arrived on the great overlook at the southern edge of the dawnlands from which the northern settlements of Massachussetts spread far and wide, a bumpy expanse of lowlands to the south.

Without a word, they filed down the mountain and swept toward Colrain, contentedly plotting the destruction of villages along the Askaskwi Sibo.

They found opportunities in several places, killing two farmers, burning their cabin and barn, slaughtering their cattle, and then moving into the edges of Northfield that evening. They murmured words of keeping on the burning structures, asking the great spirits to prevent the parasitic colonists from returning.

In the gathering shadows one evening, another farm lay

quiet, impetuously set back from the Northfield fort, behind a hill. Silently, Saksis stole up to the house, which showed a bit of candlelight through the single, small window set in the front door. From a small shed, he took a large hammer and beckoned to a group of four men, who came up to the door, ready for action. With two blows they smashed the door in, and they took the man and his wife completely by surprise. The men quickly kicked the man to the ground, pulled his head back and cut his throat while the woman screamed. They silenced her in the same fashion.

Now with four new scalps, they headed into the night, newly lit by a large quarter moon, just up over the horizon. They climbed the hill and followed a small stream to the edge of the clearing of the fort, and thirty-four men fell asleep, concealed by brush. At first light they ate a little *skamon* mash from the pouches they always carried at their belts, and watched as signs of life slowly appeared at the fort. The main gate opened, and two soldiers came out, walking lazily into the clearing toward the river.

Saksis sent a string of ten men to file carefully up along the southwest corner, where they might stay unseen. They managed this—they were soon alongside the fort, and all remained quiet. Saksis sent four men to dispatch the two by the river, as another ten crept around the fort under the muskettholes, until they lay ready by the opening. At a signal from Saksis they plunged through the gate while the remaining twenty charged toward the fort, Saksis leading.

The invaders only found thirteen men at the fort; the work proved short, their preparations effective. They killed seven defenders quickly in the brief skirmish, and two more by the river; one Alnôbak yelped, wounded in the side with a knife, though it wasn't too serious. His opponent fell quickly, skull cracked by the smooth stone of a club. Saksis covered the wound with a boiled poultice of comfrey tied around the waist; this staunched the bleeding and would purify the wound. Some of the men bound the prisoners and marched them out into the main clearing, while fifteen dawnlanders set about burning the fort. It was a fair amount of work, as the young wood stubbornly refused to catch, but in the end they damaged the palisade severely, and satisfied, they headed west again into the forest.

Many of these new captives proved fairly belligerent, even though they were completely helpless. The very first night, back up on a west-facing hillside, the warriors set up camp, and decided that with this group, it might be fun to hold a gauntlet, to soften them up a bit. Two rows of fifteen men were set up with sticks and clubs, and the remaining captors herded the six unlucky complainers one at a time through the throat of this bottleneck. The men sprinted as fast as they could, but every one took painful clips in the legs, jabs in the side, and an occasional bash across the brow. Soon they lay stretched at one end of the campsite, moaning. One at a time, the braves untied them and let them go down to a nearby hollow to get washed up. They were quite subservient now.

The rest of the march back to Pointe a la Chevalure passed quickly; along the way a *moz* was killed, and when they got back to the lake, the women prepared a celebratory feast. The soldiers, their hands still tied, sat in a row as the villagers mocked them.

"Your noble fort! What a shame! Your friends will have to cut down another two hundred trees just to calm themselves down!"

"What a fierce battle you fought! Scratched one of us a little. Better than you English usually manage!"

"I hear the food's terrible in Montreal prisons. You'll find out soon enough!"

The men glowered as the braves taunted them in English. In the morning the party borrowed two bateaux, and they all traveled north. It was fun, feeling the wind whistling past as the six British captives rowed steadily northward.

1748

Along the Wantastegok, two leagues west of Fort Dummer, Saksis and his men enjoyed a campfire, talking and pulling on long pipes of tobacco. They'd gathered ten scalps in a fortnight, and the mood became jovial as they roasted *bakesoak*, *belazak*, and *nahamak*, the results of two days' birdhunting. Jean Jacques, the Kahnawake who'd accompanied Saksis in the raid on Nehemiah Howe's fort, sat apart from the group, busy chiseling a face in a large piece of brown shale. Saksis eyed his work with interest. "Jacques, what is that—a squirrel? Look at the cheeks!"

The man was embarrassed, and his cheeks flushed as they discussed his inexpert handiwork.

"It's my uncle, Jean Baptiste. He has a round face."

"The Frenchman? I know him! He fought down here with my grandfather, in Dummer's War."

"Oh, believe me, I know. He was up on this very brook, and he carved the date into a stone. 1723."

"Really? So you're following his path."

"Yes, he was always good to me. He died last year. I want to leave a record of my family's visits here—our stamp on the battleground."

"Well, you should put the date in there."

"Don't worry! I'll start on that next."

He added more to the carving, and Saksis, watching, grew curious. "What's that, to the left of his face? And what are those lines?"

"That's his bow, and the line below the face is supposed to be his body. The other line's his arm. I wanted to put a sun or moon up there to his right, but it's just a bunch of holes right now."

"Well, Jacques, you did muff that one. It looks like rain." The two men laughed, which eased the man's embarrassment.

They ate well, and soaked in the warmth of the fire until late in the evening. Jean Jacques carved the numbers very beautifully, by comparison to the face. "Those are nicely done. Why 1745, and not 48?" Saksis wondered.

He looked sheepish. "It's a marker for the last raid I came down on. I didn't get a chance to carve it then. If we're still here tomorrow, I'll make another for this trip. As for the lettering, I know how to write well—I'm just not much of an artist."

Saksis answered, "Well, I don't know—you brought that scalp to life up on the Ktsi Mskodak in that raid!" They laughed again at the memory of the leering, red face. Then they curled up, warm enough in their layered furs and long moccasins, and fell asleep.

Saksis awoke sharply, to British voices in the hollow.

"Daniel, come on out of the woods there. We're headed to Colrain, not Crown Point!"

"I swear I saw something up there." A boy's voice.

Saksis crouched low, and shook two of his men who still lay sleeping. The other nine were already awake, aroused by the same sound, crouching, ready for action. He made a gesture, and they loaded their muskets silently. He pointed to two men, and signaled they should capture the boy. He signaled, "Take the guns. To me!" and grabbed his tomahawk and a pistol. They took positions. With a whoop, Saksis sprinted down the hill, as his men opened fire.

The boy was seized and carried away by two men, each with a forearm under one armpit, as the child's legs thrashed in futility. Jean Jacques sent a metal ball crashing through the ribs of one of the boy's companions. The others closed ranks around him and began a retreat toward Fort Dummer, loading and firing as quickly as they could, taking cover behind trees. Saksis' men kept up their fire. The brook, to the right, proved an open area with poor footing, so some kept to the path, as the others tried to flank their opponents from the left. They caught one man with a ball to the head—his neck jerked quickly and he fell, dead.

The others turned and ran, and in their quick burst covered nearly half a league. They'd almost reached the rise from which they'd see the fort, when Saksis caught one man in the back with his tomahawk. He fell toward the rear of the group, and Saksis was on him immediately, giving him a quick, merciful knife in the heart. Others bounded past him toward the only remaining man, momentarily tackled and killed.

"Nice work! Do you think they heard us at the fort?"

"I expect they did! Let's get off into the hills."

The small band turned and jogged briskly back up the trail, where they found the two men holding the boy. Without a word, they passed the trio and headed into the woods to the north, toward Wantatstekw. The boy ran toward the rear, tears on his face, pushed ahead by his captors. This is the worst part of abduction, Saksis thought. The moment of loss and separation.

Rushed along on the trail home, Jean Jacques didn't have time to carve another marker.

〰○〰

At Mazipskoik, their old friend Father Lauverjat greeted them at the jetty, calling out in French. He'd been stationed here over a year now, and everyone liked him. A kindhearted man, but a strong supporter of the war effort. An outspoken critic of the French manipulation of the people of Mazipskoiodanak. Always good to see him.

"Ahh, Sachette! What have we here?"

"Thirteen scalps and a young Englishman! Not bad for a week's work, eh?"

"The governor will be pleased. Toss the bowline." He caught it, looping it over a low dauphin, caught the stern line and pulled the boat alongside the pier as Saksis jumped ashore and made it fast, then allowed the passengers to climb out. The priest came over to him. "You'd better get up to your family compound. Your grandfather has finally taken ill."

"How long ago?"

"More than a fortnight. He's very weak."

The bateaux were made fast, and the men trudged up the main path into town. They left the weary, blond-haired boy in the custody of a few guards, who herded him into a small block-house, cut his bonds, then closed and locked the door.

Father Lauverjat looked a little uncomfortable as the prisoners were stowed, and he said, almost to himself, "Don't worry. We'll get him to a good family soon." Then, to Saksis: "What's his name?"

Saksis had questioned the boy, who remained pretty defiant despite his fear. "Dan Sargent. He's pretty old—he might not take. Better keep an eye on him. I've got to get up to see Grandfather." To three of his men, he said, "take the scalps—get the bounty. I'll see you tonight."

Two of the remaining warriors were Woronoke; another three were eastern Alnôbak refugees who lived on Wawanolewat's compound. The six men headed up past the swamps and the flint outcropping into the forest, and finally to the small *wigwôm* village where a few barking dogs heralded their arrival. Bilinto came out of his house and greeted his son with a long embrace.

"How is he?"

"Close to death. I'm sorry to tell you. The women have been by his side for days. Everyone's exhausted. But he is still awake sometimes—still speaking, barely. We should go see him now."

Saksis grew younger as he entered the long *wigwôm*, which had eleven separate family firepits, as Wawanolewat had many children who now held camp at home with their revered grandfather. Wizwame stayed close by his side, pale and peaceful. She smiled at her son as he arrived at his grandfather's bed, and he smiled back. For the last time, Kawazinamito kneeled at Wawanolewat's shoulder.

"Grandfather."

His eyes opened slowly. He turned his head and smiled, taking in the sight of his grandson, from his daughter reclaimed from his homeland of Woronoco.

"Namito, my son. You look well. I think me, not so much."

"You look brave and strong, Grandfather. You always look proud and strong to me."

"Tell me, my son. Where have you been these past days?"

"I and some of the men from our village took the new fort they had on the great meadow Ktsi Pôntekw, south of the falls. We killed one man and captured one. We destroyed the fort, and killed the cattle. After we brought the man to Pointe a la Chevalure, we returned and raided two farms. Then we took Northfield. I wish you could have been with us, great father. Only one man wounded."

The old man placed his hand on the young brave's head, "Sixty years have passed since I took your mother from my homeland. She gave me a grandson I am proud of. The people of the wooded ships should not be so numerous. They should not be so lucky, to have so many guns and such good health. They should not be in the land of your father's people. But you and the rest of our braves protect it. You keep the white men guessing, you keep them afraid, so they do not become too many. You thin the numbers, you kindle cleansing fire where they have made their boxes of wood, their houses, beds, and dinner tables. You make them leave. When they do this, say a blessing on the land so they may not return."

"I do. I utter words of keeping on the places after I've burnt them. Other men do the same."

Wawanolewat didn't seem to hear him. "These are a people of corners," the old man continued, his grey locks flowing about his deathbed. "Square houses, square furniture, sharp, square boundaries on their land. When I was a child, before we were forced to leave Woronoco, we had clear boundaries too, for hunting and cultivation—but even then, we shared with other clans. Their approach is to section the earth and own it—one man, one patch of earth. They destroy everything that is good. It seems the land should tire of being the host—they take such a small patch and work it until it's dead—no *wobimenal*, no *sogalebi* in the late winter when the earth bottom drops out, and all is mud— no roots to hold the mud, no moss to hold the water—no *wôbo-ziak*, no *awasoaks*, not even an *azeban*. I have seen them stop the creeks, too, with walls that make small lakes, like *temakwak* do— but their walls, no *mowômagw* could cross. The baby fish must die, trapped, unable to get to sea, or worse, never born, as their parents cannot find the homeland. I wonder what they would do to the Kwanitekw, these people, if we did not fight them away. Could they stop even that river?"

"The French say they could. They say there are huge walls in the rivers where they come from. They do not understand fish migration there." Saksis spoke as in disbelief, remembering his dream at Turners Falls, knowing what Wawanolewat suggested could be true. "I have seen such a wall, in a vision."

The old man had similar memories—visions of his own. He replied.

"So you have seen their wanton destruction in your dreams. You feel their poison. You braves must round their corners, and bring the circle back again. Reduce their wood to ash, their bodies to soil. Show them the old way of the land—let them join our generations, rotting beneath the earth in Sokwakiak, at the Ktsi Pôntekw, in Penacook, at Schaghticoke. These men are parasites in the wilderness, nonflowering plants with fragile stems that grow thick. They are hairy and unclean. They smell!" He smiled ruefully, and everyone laughed. "They are invasive species, forming their colonies. They do not belong here. Massasoit should never have let them in."

He went on. "Our people have lived by the *mskwamagok* in spring, and the fat of mammals and the sugar of *sogalikan* in winter. In summer, wealth is provided by the great spirit, and we work the land so in the fall we get *skamonal* to last the year." If we broke the cycle of seasons, our people would be broken. These white men threaten to break the cycle, to tear the link of *mskwamagok* and *wôbamagwsizak*. They must be stopped. You have my blessing, son, for the work you do these coming years."

"You are honored, grandfather."

Addressing the whole group, the elder explained, "I love you all. You are the people of the dawnlands and the people of the beaver. You are the keepers of the old ways, and every one of you is precious. Not just to me, but to the land, to the spirit. You are a blessed people, and every one of you carries thousands of ancestors inside you. They can be called upon for advice. You no longer need me. You can leave me now. I will go on in peace and walk the sky. Like you someday, I will walk with Glooskap and Odhihozo. I will fly with Pmola. I will visit your enemies and support your work in keeping their monstrous fire low, in the dawnlands. I fear the land of the Amiskwôlowôkoiak is overrun."

The crowd around him stirred, and some rose to leave. His partner, Marie Chantel, and the 65-year-old girl, once little Elizabeth Sackett, stayed by his side, and dabbed at his forehead with a wet cloth. Wawanolewat closed his eyes forever.

The clan of a thousand Pocumtuck and Alnôbak—a hardened people, united in respect for the passing of their warrior-poet, made a human corridor into the forest to the damp earth where Saksis, Nebilinto and five other men had dug a deep, oval resting place, and lined shelves inside with tools of hunting and war. Borne along by the women, Wawanolewat floated up the path, and was lain in his earthen bed. A survey of eyes in the crowd showed wide variation: tears, hollow loss, wise acceptance, peace and gratitude, defiance. Sometimes these visages flowed into one another, on the same faces. A profound sense of honor pervaded the entire grove, and on an unmarked hillside, in an unmarked grave, Wawanolewat moved on to other things.

Saksis turned on leather heels and walked off in the native, instepped way, feet following one another single file, his walk revealing the considerable weight of his sense of responsibility. His mission, while he remained in the world of men.

A few weeks passed, and he headed swiftly southward with his newest party. Memories traveled with the sober man as he bounded along the narrow trail, through the granite boulders of this northern pass, between crags of shale. His grandfather had been so old, no one knew his real age. He was easily over ninety, and during his long life everything had changed. Saksis' life had been similar—like Wawanolewat, he was born into a refugee's world—a world of insurrection. He'd been reared through times of peace and war. The resentments of his people were his own. Best of all, war had been declared yet again. This time it was a world war, like in 1704 when his grandfather led the great raid on Deerfield, a village British colonists had brazenly founded on the former site of the largest Pocumtuck village.

In the early spring of the previous year, Saksis became embroiled in an unsuccessful raid on Fort Four, under Chevalier Niverville. He turned that experience over in his mind, as he journeyed southeast through the mountains.

He volunteered, one of twelve dawnlanders who would guide, hunt, and scout for the French detachment. Niverville's plan was to overrun the fort with over a hundred men in the early dawn, burning as much as he could, and gaining entry by subterfuge if possible. He sent three scouts creeping down in the middle of the night, to see if they could get past the palisades and then sleep at the base of the fort alongside the wall where they would not be seen. Then in the morning, they could set up for the attack.

Saksis, François Mantok, and a third man named Mahoda were sent out late, when the moon was high, to scout the perimeter and look for entry. A light cloud cover kept them well concealed, but the pointed, vertical logs were sunk into the earth too close together to penetrate, too deep to remove. The scouts came in close, to confer.

"We could try to cut one down." Mantok was ever the optimist, and Saksis had to disagree.

"It would be too difficult to avoid drawing attention in the process." He addressed Mahoda. "What's the gate like?" He could guess already, as he had seen it many times last year, and it likely hadn't changed.

"Stout pine, four inches thick, with strong iron crosswork and hinges. Impassable." Just as he had remembered.

"Do we have any recourse here, do you think?" The men could come up with nothing.

"I'll take 'em on even if there are seventy inside." Mahoda smiled recklessly.

This pair weren't Saksis' favorite companions. They could easily get them all killed. "Don't choose to die too easily. You'll have your chance to fight," Saksis replied. "We'll do something good here tomorrow. Get some rest."

And they turned in for five quiet hours, until the birds were singing in the forest, and light began to break.

At the main camps, Niverville woke them all. "Eat. Be ready."

They all put some biscuit to soak in water, then ate it with salt pork. They combed their hair, cleaned their weapons, prepared torches and fire arrows, and waited for movement at the fort.

In the morning, the doors remained closed. The colonists moved about behind the gate, seeming nervous. Finally the gate opened, and one man let out a group of dogs, who ranged around, barking nervously. He fired his gun, and walked slowly toward the middle of the clearing, calling out to the dogs. "Sheboy! Sheboy!" The dogs could feel the tension—everyone could feel the attack impending—and even as Niverville gave the order to charge, the man turned and charged back through the heavy, wooden doorway, which slammed shut just behind him, balls thunking deafeningly into log walls all around. Avoiding enemy fire, Alnôbak men rapidly set fires by the wall, set a nearby cabin ablaze, and launched hundreds of fire arrows into the fort.

Many stuck, and began fires, but the besieged men had a well inside, and they must have worked incredibly hard, because they kept up crossfire in the field south of the fort by the front gate, somehow managing to extinguish all fires. Attempts to cut down the palisades were also repulsed. The day wore on, with no change, despite regularly renewed hostilities.

Two evenings later, Niverville called for a cessation of arms until sunrise, which was granted. He called for a parley—three men of the fort came to meet them, even as a French lieutenant, a soldier and one of the Mazipskoiak went into the fort as a temporary exchange.

"If you surrender, you can take your men, clothing, and provision, and we will leave you unharmed." He sent the men back in with this message, and asked to meet directly with Captain Stevens. As the three soldiers came out of the fort, Stevens joined them. His man Gene Debeline delivered the ultimatum: "We have seven hundred men at our disposal. It is our desire to take your fort. You have no chance. Surrender, or die. Surrender, and we will honor our terms. Refuse, and we will overrun your fort, and burn it to the ground."

Stevens replied, "I was sent by my master, our General, to defend this fort. Unless you can convince me better of these seven hundred men of which you speak, I think we are likely to take our chances. I have no assurance you will not kill us the moment we depart this place. I have only your word, and I do not know you well enough to trust you. If we have killed even one of your men, they may see fit to kill us all. We have seen greater treachery than this, and hence your offer is but poor encouragement. I will not readily risk the lives of my men."

Debeline said, "Our word is good. Bring our message to your men, and see if they have better judgment. My men eagerly await the renewal of hostility."

Stevens reentered the fort, and soon shouted his refusal from inside the walls. The attackers rallied, and redoubled their efforts, but could not get a fire to catch within the walls, despite a bombardment of hundreds of fire arrows. Eventually Niverville gave in, calling for a cease-fire, and arranging another parley the following morning. This time his terms were different—to save face, he sent Saksis and Mantok to see if they could convince Stevens to sell provisions. They set their flag of truce, and Stevens came out with one man accordingly.

After hearing the offer, Stevens explained, "Sale of provisions to a hostile army goes against our rules of engagement. But if you return all captives, we will give five bushels of *skamonal* for every man." Saksis returned to Niverville with this intelligence, whereupon he cursed Stevens roundly, and ordered his men to fire upon the fort. Frustrated, the attackers maintained their onslaught for the full course of that day and night, shouting threats and raining volleys, while the besieged men in the fort continued to wet their ramparts and dig defensive trenches. Finally, Niverville saw the situation was hopeless, short of a desperate charge which might cost half his men. He gave the order to retreat.

Mahoda would have enjoyed the charge. He became sullen, surly for a few days, as they marched down to Northfield. Saksis decided he liked him—with more like him, they might have taken the fort. He said, "Maybe we should have chopped down a palisade."

The warrior smiled wryly. "Couldn't have hurt. What's the worst that we could have done? We could have died. But what are we here for?" Saksis could find no disagreement. In the big battles, sacrifices were needed for victory. They hadn't made that sacrifice, though they lived to fight again.

A few days later, after killing only two men in Northfield, they were annoyed to hear that only thirty people had defended Fort Four.

Down south, Pinawans had more luck, successfully taking fort number two in Westmoreland with a group of fifteen men. He sent a mocking letter to the British, saying "you should commend us for caring for your repossessed settlements." This story spread through his batallion, the Frenchmen jabbering to one another about the "*sauvages courageux*," and Saksis immediately forgave the Sokwakiak somewhat for his part in selling the Ktsi Mskodak. Maybe he'd been tricked into giving up the land ten years before, but he'd repaid the British for their manipulative double talk, showing proper Alnôbak loyalty and courage.

Coming down from Manicknung, bounding over the forest floor like deer, fifty men in Saksis' newest war party traversed Wantatstekw valley in the early summer, a few leagues from the Kwanitekw.

Satak abounded, up in the hills, offering a pleasant snack. The scrub *koasak* on one peak surprised them; it appeared different from other dawnland vegetation, bare, gnarled trees on granite. There were also evergreen bushes with large leaves and white, cuplike flowers, creating a beautiful world of fresh blossoms to wander through. From the mountain's crest, which offered excellent views of Wantatstekw and the Kwanitekw valley, Saksis used his grandfather's old spyglass to spot multiple cooking fires at Fort Dummer.

While Saksis had been with his family, a few British had attempted a raid on Bitawbákw at Kwezowihomak, whereupon they were chased into the mountains and finally killed by a detachment under Sieur Louis Sablin, toward the headwaters of Wantatstekw. Relations were now hostile at best; he could follow his violent inclinations.

Saksis stuck to his course west of the fort, which he expected would be well manned—they'd avoid it, heading back into settlements west of Northfield to visit destruction upon the colonists. Konnegwak, dressed in *nolk*skin leggings and a sleeveless shirt of heavy, red cotton, joined him on the granite ridge, his ponytail a plaything of the gentle mountain breezes. Saksis kept his hair shorter, and wore a sleeveless *nolk*skin tunic and leggings. Both had soft, comfortable moccasins. The granite outcroppings made a fine setting for an afternoon rest. On the northwest face, the men made *gogowibagwok* tea. They boiled *skamonal*, mixed in piles of the delicious *satak* that covered the forest floor, and feasted.

Konnegwak suggested a run to the west, further toward Stockbridge. "Alnôbak families remain there, and they may leave to join us."

Saksis did not look pleased with the idea. "The dawnland fight has always been with Massachussetts, the Pilgrims, and you're talking about the border of New York. We'd like as not be burning out the Dutch," he replied. "Then when the people of New York rise against us, we'd be flanked across Bitawbákw, and that'd be the end. Plus, the same Algonkian families would soon be persecuted."

"All right, you're right." Konnegwak could see the reason in that. "The old places, then? Colrain, Northfield, Deerfield?"

"Yes. But I'd like to make one strike down to Woronoco, in honor of Wawanolewat. Then, back up to the Number Four blockhouse, and then, up toward Koasek."

"Very well." The afternoon wore on, and they stashed their cooking pot and a few other items under one of many fine nooks up on this mountain, strewn with granite slabs. So many comfortable places to sleep on this rocky slope! Another day...

They clambered down the west side and followed the Wantatstekw for a short way, then broke off southwest, well clear of Fort Dummer. Late morning of the following day found them perched like hawks on the great overlook, preparing another strike on Northfield.

They headed down more to the southeast along a well-beaten path, and after three leagues the men at the head of their group froze, suddenly hearing boots marching in the leaves ahead of them, and loud voices from over the hill. Everyone fell out silently into the surrounding trees, and waited. No one came, and they determined the men were headed the same way they were, to the southwest.

Up over the ridge they surveyed a group of soldiers, about forty-five—the numbers looked very similar to their own. The dawnlanders signaled to one another that they would engage. They closed in silently upon the rear guard. As they formed an enclosure, Saksis ululated, and his men fired once and charged in. They hit five right off, but the soldiers regrouped amazingly well, reacting immediately and fiercely, with knives and musket stocks. They turned and formed two lines along the path facing the trees in opposite directions, and between them a third line readied muskets for firing.

Just before the command to fire, Saksis yipped a brief falling back command, and the attackers leaped back between the trees and moved through the wood to flank the pack of soldiers, as they let loose their volley. Only two men were hit, and Saksis dug in to the front of the pack, determined to hold the ground if a countercharge came. Instead the soldiers dug in as well, with a slightly higher position, thus gaining a bit of an advantage. They had the greater firepower, as every man carried a Brown Bess, while Saksis' group had only thirty-three muskets and few pistols. The groups exchanged shots, and a few men fell on both sides, but neither gained ground.

Both commanders were reluctant to commit to a full-on battle. "Their firepower is much greater," one of Saksis' men pointed out.

"Parker! You seen 'em? What're the numbers?" Hunkered down along the trail, Captain Humphrey Hobbs addressed a soldier from the back of the line, where the attack began.

Lt. Isaac Parker, himself a former captive, replied. "At least seventy, Captain! If you'll forgive me, I'd suggest we fight another day, if we can choose. We've already lost Sam Green, Eli, and Ebenezer. Nathan and Ralph are hit. Dan and Sam Graves are pretty bad off—Sam lost some of his brains." Others who had seen the wounded men shared the lieutenant's sentiments.

Saksis also understood the reality of this encounter. His men were just overmatched in numbers, but the excellent cover of the woods made up for the lesser weaponry of the dawnlanders. Hobbs had a decent position, with higher ground which he would defend vigorously. A knoll provided his men some cover. They were deadlocked, and any attack would see heavy casualties. After twenty minutes of scattered exchange of fire, during which one of Saksis' men took a ball in the neck, Hobbs sent stentorian words flying down the hill during a lull in the action.

"What group holds the trail? We are fifty men out of Fort Dummer, headed for Fort Shirley, and we will make our way whether you like it or no."

Saksis called back. "I am Sachette, and we have numbers to match yours, and then some. Attempt the trail if you like! We'll see who masters it. We have tomahawks for all your men."

"Sackett!" The voice showed recognition. "It's Captain Humphrey Hobbs, second in command at Fort Four. I know you from trading in better times. Remember me?"

"I know you well! Good day to you, man!" came Saksis' reply. He signaled to one of his men, to tie a tump line to the fallen man's foot. They began to drag him across the forest floor, reclaiming his body.

Hobbs' voice came again. "I know also the damage you've done up to Putney, and in Northfield, and unless I'm mistaken, you attempted Fort Dummer not long ago. I hold you in respect, but your scalp would be an excellent prize! Shall we have at it?"

"Be careful your child doesn't fall into the fire." Saksis was game for a fight. "Come on down among our ranks, and we'll see what we can do for you."

"We'd have you come up to ours!"

"Likely not! With your weapons and higher ground, we'd fall quickly. We'll wait for you."

Things quieted for a few hours, and shots were fired with intermittent sniping, but the main body of soldiers never came. When dusk began to fall, three scouts circled round and learned that the soldiers were in surprisingly quiet retreat, and bulk of the troops already lay a full league away.

The dawnlanders decided to pull to the north a bit and camp on the ridge. Four men lay dead. Two were badly injured, and would not live. Another, shot in the arm, looked stoic as they dug out the ball with the blade of a knife, and merely closed his eyes as they staunched the wound with boiling water and witch hazel, which grew plentifully by a nearby stream. They tied the wound tightly—he would be fine. The others they nursed through a few hours, gave them water, and saw their spirits across the border, into other realms.

"Make frames. We'll bury them on the banks of the river."

They carried all the bodies down, and dug six deep holes scattered in a *wôbimiziak* grove, near a beautiful, rocky stream that cascaded down into Wantatstekw. The men were silent, but Saksis spoke at last. "*Ntona Ktsi Niwaskw*. Accept them, our creator. Carry them on into the spirit realm." Together, they remembered their friends. For a long time, they stood silent.

Then they considered practical matters. They decided to send the wounded man back to Pointe a la Chevalure with two others to help him. That left forty-one in the group, but their location was known, now and they felt sure a larger party would come for them in the morning from Fort Dummer. Wasting no time, the larger group headed back north, and soon raced along Wantatstekw, and crossed the ridge west of Saksis' brook, over a pinnacle covered in *zegweskimenak* berries, which provided a fine repast mixed with *skamonal*, roasted inside *bakesoak* and *belazak* they came upon, and harvested from the river valley. They considered their next move as they rotated the birds on their spits. Seven men with fourteen forked sticks turned the birds over seven fires. Over dinner, they talked of stealing over the hill to scout Fort Dummer.

They crossed the Kwanitekw late that night above the Ashuelot, and looked down upon the fort from Wantatstekw in the early light after a few hours' rest.

Suddenly, Konnegwak stretched out his arm, his palm flat, with all five fingers pointing as one. He whispered, "Look there!"

Saksis followed the line of his outstretched arm to a line of small shapes moving along the eastern bank, above the riverbend, southward to the fort. They couldn't have been more than twenty.

"Perfect." He called to the men, who formed an attack wing, beginning a sweep down through the wood. They fell upon the men like a wind, and with two men to each of the British, it was over in a heartbeat. The colonists turned, and their faces broadcast fear as they shouted, and alternately scampered or tried to mount a defense. One of the bravest died quickly, skull cloven by a hatchet. Six managed to dive in the river and swim away—two others were killed in the water, and two more were hit, though they kept going. The dawnlanders captured eleven, and tied their hands with leather straps.

Time was precious. So much to be accomplished. "Run fast as you can, or we'll kill you!" Saksis was serious this time, and drove the captives like an angry sheepdog. They made excellent time due north along the river, crossing well below the Ktsi Mskodak. They disappeared into the hills, and surfaced again at Fort St. Frederic in four days with their captives.

1753

In midsummer, after gathering fish and hunting, Saksis organized another raiding party. They met in the wood and headed west toward the Kwanitekw again, toward the uplands. Peace had reigned for a time, but the men were pleased to feel the British/French relations shaken once again, and the French in Chambly hoisted the flag of war, their old friend. Saksis and a party of men from the compound were happy to oblige, and they sat in the warm, hazy shade of an *anaskawezi*, preparing weapons and talking. They considered their opponents.

"Ahh, Stevens. He could be a thorn." Konnegwak remembered the stern truckmaster, a captive of Wawanolewat's when just a boy. He had impressed them all a few years earlier, during the siege.

"Yes, he'll be a tough nut. With luck, he won't have many men. They won't be ready for us—this will be the first attack this round, and we'll startle them. I feel sure of it." Saksis felt brightly optimistic as he contemplated the damage he could do with an element of surprise.

With just sixteen men this time, he traveled nearly single file through the pass of Onegígwizibó and down the ridge to Wantatstekw, which they followed until it grew to a width of three rods, southwest of Manicknung. Word had come to the party of names like Kathan, Willard and Minott; families who dared once again to settle and farm up above Sokwakiak, near the Ktsi Mskodak, below the falls. They had carved a fort out of the trees just south of the meadow, and Saksis meant to visit them and wreak some havoc. The new town on his family's brook, called

Putney, lay just over the ridge. The men climbed the ridge and spent two nights near the stone chamber his family had lived in when he was a small boy, along the brook just two miles west of the new settlement on the Kwanitekw. Saksis still kept grain, a cooking pot, and weapons there, safely hidden in their old root cellar. Well-fed, their arms renewed, the small party crept toward the small blockhouse in the late summer evening. As night fell, they stole through the long shadows, as they had when taking Northfield ten years earlier.

Suddenly, a cry went up from inside the fort. They were seen. They fell back, as shots began to ring out, and fortifications were quickly set up inside the blockhouse. The crew quickly stoked a small fire, and launched fire arrows, rolled with crackling *mask-wak* bark and cotton cloth, into the structure. Nothing caught, and in the end, the group fell back. They spread out through the area, and managed to destroy a few small fields of *skamonal*, and burned a barn set up near the fort for hay and wood. Accepting the limited results of their incursions, they started upriver.

This turned out to be a good choice. They discovered a Mohican on the trail, in the employ of Nate Willard of Fort Dummer. After they wrestled him to the ground, he saw the grim eyes of the war party, and proved very willing to talk. "Stevens is marching this morning with most of his garrison to Fort Dummer; they are probably just an hour's march north of Fort Putney. I'm scouting the trail for them right now."

"What are all these colonists doing here?" Saksis wanted an explanation for the expansion.

"Benning Wentworth. Governor of New Hampshire. New fortifications are springing up everywhere. The governor decided this land was his to sell, and convinced hundreds of Massachusetts people to clear the land, and settle it." This news came unwelcome to Saksis. Frustrating. It seemed there were eight newly palisaded villages along the Kwanitekw, and large detachments of soldiers at every major fort.

"Damn."

Among the braves, the strong sentiment was to see how many captives they could get from the Fort Four area, since Stevens was away. Saksis was inclined this way as well. They could head a little west and sidestep the experienced Stevens as he headed south. Saksis felt confident that even if news caught up to him, he'd be far too late to rescue a missing family, even if he came in canoes at first light, which he probably wouldn't in any case. All signs pointed to a successful raid on Fort Four. A boy of sixteen, Skewedasiz, looked excited, almost nervous. The rest appeared calm and predatory.

In the morning, they ranged quickly upriver until, in the late afternoon, they could see the spiked posts of the fort from across the water. They swam across, north of the fort, and came to the edge of the trees where they lay waiting, watching like a pack of highly intelligent *molsem*. The Kwanitekw refreshed them after their day's run, and they relaxed in the forest on the eastern bank. With one man alert for danger, they munched leafy greens and *skamonal* mash, resting in the shade, renewing their energy. When darkness fell they stole ripe melons from the farm, gorged themselves, and then they all slept well on leafy beds, shrouded with soft *alnizediak* branches.

Saksis announced, "There's a farmhouse just over the ridge. We'll wait in the woods until the door is open. Then, we'll mount an attack." They spent a quiet time cleaning and loading pistols, sharpening blades, watching from behind a small rise of land east of the modest dwelling which lay calm, reflecting the dawning sun.

Melon beds lay sprawling in rows near the front of the cottage. A man came along the road, carrying a hoe, walked up the front path and knocked at the front door. A woman opened it, and he went in, leaving the door standing open.

"Yip!" Saksis and his men charged at the signal, sprinting silently toward the house from one corner, pistols and tomahawks at the ready. They were upon the man inside almost before they knew what was happening, and the surrender was immediate. Two men they found still abed upstairs, and three children were as well, two young girls and a boy of about seven. The men were all quickly tied by the wrists, and marched out to the edge of the wood where they were seated. Another girl, a teenager, started up from her stool, and they seized her and shoved her toward the door. Another woman, the matron of the house, and her children stood naked, terrified, standing in a cluster in the front room where the raiding party had brought them. Saksis seized a pile of laundered gowns, and handed them to the extremely pregnant woman, ripe with child, like one of the melons in her dooryard.

"Don't kill us!" She begged for their lives, as she wrapped a gown about her, and wrapped her children, who stood blinking, dumbstruck.

"Woman, if you can make it on the trail, none of you will die." Saksis tried to be reassuring, but it would be a tough trail for her, he knew. But a newborn child. A definite, new member of the community, if it lived. Saksis decided they'd take good care of her.

"I need a petticoat as well. That one there." Saksis eyed the frumpy coat with its buttons and loops of ribbon. It would be like a soft thornbush, grabbing at everything near it on the trail.

"No, I think not. Warm weather." He gestured to the air. "Your gown will do." The woman proceeded to tie it around her waist. Konnegwak stood by her—he had pulled her from her bed, where she had clutched at the posts, unwilling to go, and as a result she became his official charge.

"Let's hear your names!" Saksis issued the order to the seated group.

One by one, the men called out their names.

"Farnsworth."

"Johnson. This is my wife and children." He pointed to the gowned, motley group huddled together at the edge of the garden.

"Labarree."

"And your name, miss?" Saksis addressed the young woman.

"Miriam Willard. I'm Susannah's sister, there." She indicated the pregnant woman.

Saksis spoke in Alnôbak. "Willard is second in command at the fort. These must be his daughters. I know him, and Stevens is no coward. We'll need to move out quickly. They'll be after us as soon as they know." He addressed the men who captured specific prisoners. "All you men with the captives are to come with me. You others—" he motioned to five other men who stood empty-handed—"get off downriver, and see what you can do on your own." Addressing one of the five, he said, "Tiskwodi—you're in charge of this new party." The man smiled, and glanced around at his new group. They sprinted off for the hills, east, and then, no doubt, south toward and along the Ashuelot, to do their mischief by the old haunts near Sokwakiak.

The rest started up the trail. "No more English!" Saksis warned. "From this point on, we speak dawnlander." His small group didn't need any information sharing, or escape plotting among the captives.

The captors gathered up some small stores of food, two kettles and a few bolts of linen, a few knives and an axe. They took two muskets and a pistol, and the dry powder horn. Wrapping these things hastily in a bolt of cloth, they headed quickly into the woods. A few rods in, two of the captives, Johnson and Farnsworth, muttered quietly to each other about "food in the cellar."

"Quiet!" Saksis silenced them. He turned to Konnegwak, who stood at his right, and continued in Alnôbak. "Get back to the house, and see if there's a cellar with more food. Bring it here, quickly. We don't have much time before we're discovered, so don't look around more than a minute." Konnegwak rushed off, back toward the cottage, while the rest of the party distributed the goods from the cloth sack, and quickly made everything more portable.

Konnegwak rushed back up the path in distress. "We were seen. A man came out of the cabin, just as I came into view. He saw me, and I chased him, but he got close to the fort, and I turned and ran back here."

"Quick! We go." Saksis gave the command, and no one hesitated. "Munch!" They shoved the prisoners, hoisted the two youngest children, and everyone left at a run. Saksis herded them into single file, and led them off the trail, bushwhacking up a hillside. They headed east and south, to the Mkazawitekw.

Brambles and branches clung at them, and the captives complained noisily. Saksis whipped one across the face with a switch, and gave him a look. They fell silent. Konnegwak and Jean-Claude Alnai, a Mazipskoiak, continued to help the pregnant woman, who lost a shoe after a few minutes of scrambling. "Idiot woman." Saksis muttered under his breath. They could not go back for it.

The woman soon stopped to draw breath, winded. Her gown was tied in three places with large loops, which Konnegwak clearly felt hindered her progress, as he took out his knife and cut two of the unnecessary bands away. Her bare foot showed a large, red scratch along the instep. The woman's eyes widened at the sight of the blade; her body stiffened as he cut, then relaxed as he put it away. Clearly, she feared for her life. Konnegwak kindly patted his hilt, showing he meant no harm.

A cannon sounded from the fort, followed by a scattered crackle of musketry. A warning gun, and its answers.

"Let's get moving," Saksis said to his men. "We have a good start, and I don't think they can track us. Still, we'll put some miles on before afternoon." They headed northeast now, following the wooded ridgeline on the north side of the river where the open, rocky hilltops would not hinder their progress.

About five leagues upriver one of the children started to cry, and Saksis called a halt for a rest. He untied Johnson, and gestured toward the children, for him to see to their needs. He explained to Skwedasiz, "These people are weak, and want food. They eat three times a day, and they're not used to travel as we are. Let's unpack the easy, quick foodstuffs." Unrolling two of the bundles, the boy took out bread, some apples and raisins, and passed them among the prisoners. Saksis' own men merely tasted the raisins. They would have no need of food for another day or more.

While they ate, they heard hoofbeats along the trail, down below them. This startled them mightily, and Saksis quickly dispatched three men to scout the situation. Soon they returned, smiling. "A horse has come up behind us! All alone. No people. Shall we kill it?"

Saksis thought about this. The meat could feed them for days, but would they want to carry the meat across the river and up into the mountains? While the horse was alive, it could be useful. It could carry the pregnant woman, her foot now fully scratched and painful-looking. The captive Labarree washed it for her, and put his own stocking on her bare leg.

"No. Capture the horse. Tie it to a tree. It will serve us." The men left to do his bidding, and soon returned.

"It's a fair, well-behaved animal. No trouble."

"Okay, this woman's feet need help. Will one of you give a pair of moccasins?" Three men volunteered, and Saksis took a pair of moccasins from the closest. They handed them to Labarree, who tied them on the woman's feet. The group descended to the trail, where the horse stood waiting.

One of the captives exclaimed, "Why, it's Scoggin! Cap'n Stevens' horse!" Saksis puzzled at the presence of this animal. Strange that it belonged to the commander. But then, maybe he had a lot of horses. They had a good view of the stretch of river below them, and no sign of pursuit. Oh well—better move on. They threw blankets and the cloth across its back, and hoisted poor Susannah Johnson into the makeshift saddle.

After this repast they drove the group onward, about ten leagues further north, to a wide, relatively shallow place where the water moved lazily and they felt safe to cross. A large stand of tree branches lay massed in a small cove, and they hastily broke them up and lashed them together to float the woman across. Saksis sent Farnsworth and two of his men across first, and indicated that Labarree should swim the horse next. Saksis sent a few more of his men with Susannah Johnson clinging to a small raft, with her husband swimming alongside. Finally the children crossed with Konnegwak and the remainder of the group. Saksis swam across, last.

As he climbed the bank, he smiled, feeling completely free from pursuit. "Let's head up over this rise, and make camp here." They made a fire in a hollow of the western shore, and unrolled their small store of spoils. They set the kettles to boil, and dropped in a variety of nuts and grain. The men shared Saksis' glee, and they let out long whoops, which echoed from across the river. Later that night, with the men's feet hobbled with lashed sticks tied to a high tree branch, and the teenager roped to the ground between two men lying on the cords, a steady silence imposed itself as the captives finally seemed resigned to their predicament.

In the grey morning, an intermittent light rain misting the sky, they shared thin *skamonal* porridge, then made the prisoners march. With the pregnant woman again on horseback they traveled upland, along the Mkazawitekw, into the foothills of Ascutney. Six miles up into the hills, the two male prisoners carried the girls—but even on the horse, the woman wasn't doing so well. Regular contractions seized her, and it seemed her time for birth had come. This was unexpected.

"We need to get to the brook." Saksis didn't know much about what they'd need to do, but he did know it would be messy. They came downslope a bit, to a narrow stretch of the Mkazawitekw headwaters.

"Make the *phanem* a *wigwôm*." The men were happy to oblige, feeling birth was something a woman did, separate from others. But clearly, she could not do this on her own. They brought a skin of water, and Saksis and Miram discussed the situation; she agreed she would remain with Susannah through the ordeal. The husband also asked to join her, and Saksis assented. They waited at some distance with the children, listening to the woman's cries and moans.

The small children cried; finally, the four-year old spoke to the older boy. "Sylvanus, is she going to be okay?"

"She'll be fine, don't worry," came the reply. They fell silent again, and rain began to drizzle, bringing a chill. They all huddled in their gowns, looking miserable. Finally, an infantile cry rang out in the forest.

The woman seemed reasonably well, though exhausted, and everyone felt happy. The new child brought a warm feeling, despite the captives' glum disposition. Konnegwak was elated. He grinned at the family, and danced about a bit, chanting in his poor English, "Two monies for me!" He meant the bounty paid for captives—his one payment had changed to two.

Saksis smiled wryly. "Yes, you're lucky I guess. If it lives!" He added, "Anyway, they're you're work now. I want her on the trail again tomorrow. You can carry the baby if you have to."

Konnegwak seemed to realize what he had taken on. "Let her rest the afternoon. We can make a litter to carry her for a while. The prisoners can carry her."

"No problem. I figured on that anyway. Pull the men together. Get some branches, some straight, some feathery. Make the litter. We'll give her a new shelter for the night. I'll make it myself." Konnegwak went off to find some straight branches while others brought *alnizediak* boughs to Saksis, who wove a new, clean shelter under a spreading *senemozi,* with fresh, dry leaves and a soft, green roof and floor. Labaree and Johnson brought her up, and after she lay about nursing the child, she hungrily ate ten *skamonal* cakes and a handful of *bagônol* off a bark plate, drank a quart of water, and fell hard asleep. Neither she nor the child awoke until the next morning, as far as Saksis could tell.

The men carried her for hours, into the afternoon—Labaree, Johnson, and Farnsworth. Finally they were exhausted, and they set her down by a stream, a headwater of the Mkazawitekw. As they lay about miserably, Susannah suggested to Saksis, "If you let me ride on the horse, I think I'll make it. These men are done with this activity, I think."

Saksis smiled at her, impressed with her fortitude. She looked exhausted herself. "Okay. Your husband can carry the baby."

They hoisted her carefully up onto Scoggin, and set off soon after, the colonists plodding up the hillsides, spurred on by their captors. They had to stop periodically to let Susannah rest—the bumpy ride did not leave her in a good way. Still, they made it through the next day, a ragged pull through rocky mountains, with Johnson taking excellent care of the baby. By the time the land tilted toward Bitawbákw, they staggered unsteadily, badly in need of nourishment.

Saksis sent out hunting parties. "Check the rocky caves, and the streams. Bring what you can." The hunters came back in three hours, with only a couple of robins, and a kettle they found stashed in one of the caves. Saksis made the decision. "We'll kill the horse."

The men were pleased. So this would become a feast day, then. They stayed, they cooked, they ate. Their fire horn, with its dry tinder and Mazipskoik chert, served to quickly build a cheerful blaze; dry wood abounded. The men carved up and handed out meat for broiling. They made a rack and hung strips, and lay spits across. Soon there was food aplenty, and Saksis thanked the great spirit for sending them the horse—first it carried the mother, and now it would feed their famished party, which could hardly stand. This meat would last two days, easily.

Saksis knew the captives would fare poorly, unless they were careful. European stomachs weren't used to the all-at-once-every-few-days approach the Alnôbak observed on the trail. He brought the nutritious liver and kidneys over to the new mother, and made a show of carving them up and giving them out to all the captives, only giving them a little at a time. Susannah Johnson seemed grateful. The children ate rapidly, and Saksis made gestures to them to slow down, or their stomachs would be sore. They watched him, and looked at their mother. She didn't assert herself, apparently feeling they hadn't had enough these past few days, and this was a rare opportunity. They continued to eat wolfishly.

Saksis took up the first round of gnawed bones and cracked them, making a broth which he offered to Susannah. She took it gratefully, and sipped slowly through the evening, nursing her child.

Soon everyone felt well again, and the mood became festive. Konnegwak danced around, and sang a song about the spirits of the mountains, which he invented as he danced:

Spirits of the mountain
Old pine trees, you *koasak abaziak*
Spirit of the mountain
Look at me!
I am dancing.
Great Spirit, we know you are here
We know that you are watching us.
We honor you.
You have given us plenty.

Saksis chuckled to himself, imagining what the captives must think of the song and dance.

Before sleeping, the two little girls and the boy became sick, complaining of sore stomachs. They punctuated the night with their moans, and their trips into the nearby forest. As a result Saksis and Susannah did not sleep well, though most of the men slept soundly.

In the morning the little ones slept late, finally purged of their evening meal. Saksis sent men out for herbs and vegetables, and set Konnegwak to start a pot to boil while he cracked the big leg bones for a marrow stew. Shortly men came back with handfuls of tender, washed *alnôbai dipwabel* and *winozak*, and Saksis cut it up and boiled it with the precious salt he carried in his pouch. When the meal came ready, the children were awake, and all were grateful for this gentle, hot, nourishing breakfast. When they finished, Saksis gave the order. "Munch!"

The kids remained ill from the feasting; Farnsworth had to carry one, and Konnegwak the other. Labarree carried the infant. Later in the day, Susannah Johnson struggled. Along the riverbed, headed down a steep valley, she fainted. Miriam Willard climbed down the rocky bank to dip her pocket kerchief in the stream, and was headed back toward her sister when Konnegwak spied Jean-Claude walking toward the collapsed woman with his tomahawk out.

"Jean-Claude! You cannot!"

His voice was even as the reply came: "She's slowing us down."

"Saksis!"

Watching them through the trees, Saksis let out a fox call, to summon the men to a meeting. They sat the prisoners in a circle where they could watch them, and held an impromptu council.

Jean-Claude felt entirely justified. "She isn't going to make it. Konnegwak has the child, and so his bounty is the same as ours. It isn't fair to us. We're all losing time here."

Saksis saw his point, but he had come to admire the woman's fortitude. "If she can be aroused, and make it through today's march, we'll see what tomorrow brings. If she falls twice more, we kill her."

Konnegwak looked dismayed. He knew his personal gain wasn't a selling point, so he played up her courage and strength. "She's a good woman. She'll make it okay."

By this time Susannah Johnson lay awake, with Miriam at her side. She sat up, listening to the men discuss her fate in their strange language. When they stood, Miriam looked terrified. She had seen the raised tomahawk, and knew what they were talking about. Her eyes averted, she directed words to the seated men.

"She can make it. She just had a spell. Don't worry about her. Come on, sister. Put your arm on my shoulder." She suddenly glanced up at Saksis, and he gave her a look that explained everything. Konnegwak said, "That horse helped a lot. Maybe the men can carry her."

They started off again at a slow pace. Saksis saw Miriam whispering to her sister, whose eyes grew wide, and she seemed suddenly invigorated. Susannah even smiled at him—the forced smile of a captive, fighting for survival.

Skwedasiz didn't make it much easier. He enjoyed picking on Miriam, and kept making comments about her, pulling her hair. She snapped at him a few times. Johnson came alongside his wife, and held her up. Finally, she tripped and fell.

Konnegwak ran toward the couple with his tomahawk drawn, scaring them terribly. He merely sidestepped them and started hacking at the bark of a fallen *maskwamozi* by the trail. Cutting a large square, he showed Johnson how to set it on his shoulders to make a pack saddle for his wife. He was weary, but willing, and carried the woman through the mountains for about fifteen leagues, until they made camp that night. By this time, they'd crossed from the headwaters of the Mkazawitekw to the Onegígwizibó. They made a small bower for the nursing mother, and everyone went quickly to sleep. Johnson, completely spent, lay motionless like a dead creature.

In the morning they had horse steaks again. They were entering the extensive *temakwak* fields, crunching a few leagues of white, gnawed branches underfoot. Eventually they came to a portion of stream they needed to ford, about fifteen feet wide. Johnson carried the baby, and Farnsworth and Larrabee carried the children over. After entering the water, Susannah Johnson seemed to get disoriented. Johnson set the baby down and waded into the pool, helping his wife across. She collapsed on the other side.

"She's exhausted." Konnegwak offered an obvious analysis.

"Let's hold up here. We can build a fire and rest for a couple hours." Saksis' words relieved Konnegwak and the captives.

Dry kindling abounded, and soon they had a small fire going.

Susannah Johnson's spirits improved dramatically, and in two hours they hit the trail again, with Johnson chosen to carry his wife. Konnegwak saddled him up, and Saksis told the rest to "munch."

He spent that day scouting up ahead of the party, tired of marching with them. Taking Skwedasiz with him to lessen the tension for the women, they ran off ahead, and came to a wide tributary of the Onegígwizibó. They stripped and swam, enjoying the wide, deep water of the long, jagged pool, with fingers in hundreds of hollows. He could see a flapping of wings in one—a brace of *gwigwigemok*, looked like. Saksis signaled to Skwedasiz above the water, and they moved slowly toward the inlet. With about a hundred feet to go, the swimmers submerged and rapidly advanced in eight feet of water, until they could see the webbed feet kicking in the sunlight above. Together they advanced, but one of the birds must have caught a shadow as it peered down at Saksis right as he came up, then kicked frantically as it took off, eluding him. Skwedasiz had better luck, coming away with a flapping, unhappy *gwigwig*. He quickly wrung its neck.

They swam to shore and walked back toward the trail, hearing the voices of their prisoner party coming down the hill as they went. They met up with Konnegwak and the others, and found a good area for a fire. They roasted the bird, made some broth with the plentiful *dipwabel* and *winozak*, and prepared to share it out amongst them all.

Saksis asked Konnegwak, "How's the mother been?"

"A real pain. She is weak, but she's been complaining constantly."

Skwedasiz said, "Let's give her the head, and see what she does with it."

"Yeah! What the hell," said Konnegwak. "What she really needs the broth anyway, and we'll give her plenty of that."

So they served her a bowl of broth with the *gwigwig* head floating in it. As expected, she recoiled, but surprisingly remained silent. She withdrew to a small stand of soft *alnizediak*, and poked around in her bowl for a while. Finally she flipped the head over the side and drank the rest away.

"Did you see the look on her face?" Konnegwak and

Skewedasiz would joke about this for days. "Tomorrow we'll be at our camp. There is plenty of food for all of us."

The next two days were uneventful. The prisoners remained weak, but okay. They feasted on vegetable stew with *awaso-sibemi*, bear fat, the next day at camp, and caught some large rodents, the *agaskwok*, in the meadows on the way down to Kwezowihomak, where foods were always plentiful in the deep waters of Bitawbákw.

On the lake, they had to worry about the Yorkers, coming and going everywhere. The men didn't want their prisoners seen, so they made them lie in the bottom of the canoes as they headed up to Fort St. Frederic.

1759

Inevitably, Fort St. Frederic fell to General Jeffrey Amherst, though French hammers and fire wasted the building before the men retreated north in their blue waistcoats, white justaucorps and black trihorn hats. The British stonemasons now labored to build a new fort they called Crown Point. Up at the old compound, Saksis kept hosting refugees, flowing in from the south, and even now, from the north. Two days before, over three hundred appeared suddenly, escaping the evil Captain Rogers, who had attempted a major raid on Odanak. A very bad sign for the French and English war, and for the Alnôbak peoples, that the British could now strike so close to the heart of their people. Mazipskoik would only be a temporary refuge. Deep in the woods, commanding his grandfather's palisade, Saksis took in twenty-three from this sad stream of humanity.

Despite the 'major victory' for the British, the truth remained that once again, most of the Alnôbak had slipped through their fingers. Visiting refugees told stories of the escape. In the end Rogers killed about forty, mostly women and children, despite orders from General Amherst not to do that. Meanwhile, word went out that the arrogant aggressor loudly proclaimed his men had "wiped out the town," killing "over two hundred."

Saksis asked of his uncle Noluwey, now a chief at Odanak. "He's fine," a woman named Melicomka responded. "They got away."

The Odanak woman told this story. "We were at the council house, dancing. Samadagwis, a Schaghticoke Mohican, came up to my daughter, outside the house, and spoke in a southern dialect, the language of our people: *"Ndapsizak kedôdemôkawleba;*

kwawimleba. Kedatsowi wakwatahogaba. My friends, I am telling you, I would warn you. They are going to exterminate you." A few there smiled at her imitation of the man's pronunciation.

Melicomka smiled, and continued. "Samadagwis went on: 'Don't be afraid. I am your friend, and your enemies are in the woods, planning that when all the Alnôbak leave for home, they will kill them all, their husbands, and burn your village, and I come to warn you.' My daughter came in and told me, and I believed her. Thank God." She crossed herself. "Anyway, word spread quick, and we were able to get our stuff and get out of town within half an hour. Most people went to hide in the *koasak*, a ravine not far from town—a great hiding place we call Sibosek. Over a hundred of us stayed there, quiet and waiting. We bided our time for more than a day, until our scouts told us we were safe. But the loss is great, my brothers and sisters. Odanak is in ruins. Our houses, and our history. The church records are gone."

Another refugee, Gabriel Annance, had a similar story. "My kids saw him too. Samadagwis. He saved them. I sent them out quick into the bushes right as Rogers' men started to come through the forest, and I went to lead them another way. But one crossed toward their path, and the Mohican told my little girl to run. Then he took aim from one knee, and shot the Englishman. Others came running, but found only him, and my kids got away. I'm sure they killed him."

A healthy young man named Panadis spoke up. "Oh, they did. I was among those who returned the next day." He told of the losses. "Some thirty were killed, who didn't believe us, and stayed at home. Foolish. A few wary unbelievers were late, and when they saw the soldiers coming, they ran. Most got caught. Obomsawin, he came just before dawn, across the river. I saw him. Just as he crossed, the light shone and flashed on his silver maskwas cap. And just like that, they were there, and they saw him. Four started firing, and they got him. We found him on the riverbank later, and buried him. It were a big burial, and my back still aches from cutting the earth."

Then Panadis told his story of the Schaghticoke messenger. "We also found Samadagwis by the side of the road. He was mortally wounded, and lay dying. We offered to kill him, as he was in grievous pain. He said "Don't kill me yet. I am not baptized yet."

"What is your name?" I said.

"Samadagwis. I am Mohican."

"Is this how you want to be baptized?"

"No."

"What name should we give you?" I asked.

"Sabadis. Jean Baptiste."

"And so I sprinkled water on him, and crossed him on his forehead, and kissed, and called him by his new name. He looked at peace. A few moments later one of us put him away, quick and easy, with a hatchet. We knew him for our savior, the day before, and we honored him in proper burial. He was truly loyal."

Saksis offered, "I wonder if he were traveling with Rogers. If he were one of them."

"If so, he was put there by God to save us." Panadis would have no soil on the man's memory. "Maybe he came with them, the whole time, planning to inform us all along. Maybe he came to hate the men he was traveling with, or he came to hate Rogers, for whatever reason. Maybe his guilt just got the better of him, the day before the massacre. Or maybe he was just traveling north on Bitawbákw, saw them coming, and sprinted ahead of them for our sake. Whatever his reasons, he made it possible for us all to live, the people you see before you today."

"Bless him, then. And you are welcome here. I bid you all good night, and sleep well." Saksis went off to his *wigwôm*, and left the group talking around the campfire, by their little colony of lean-tos.

He found his mother ladling hot water into a bowl of dried nettles. She seemed tired all the time, now, and Gihla cared for her. He did not think Zwame would last the winter, and he couldn't imagine living without her. He reached sixty, himself, this year, and her years reached past eighty.

"So what happened?" Her voice showed resignation, and she had not missed the significance of a British invasion of Odanak. "Is it over? Have they won?"

"I think pretty much, yes."

"But most of the people escaped."

"Yes, thanks to a Mohican who warned them. We were lucky for him. We'll sing songs for him tomorrow evening, I'm sure. A man named Samadagwis."

"Will we have to leave soon? Will the British come and take our land?" She was still a Woronoke girl at heart, despite her creamy skin. Her hairs were finally silver, matching many elders in the community. Her heart was all first nation.

"I don't know. I think probably. I don't think it would be wise to fight. The French can't protect us anymore. They're going to lose—they have lost."

Gihla spoke up. "What do you think our people should do? We've seen what happens down south, in the Pocumtuck lands. The destruction of the forests. We can't stop that now, I guess. But how can we survive as a people?" She was like a child, asking how to fix some broken toy. But it was a big question she was asking.

"Well, some will go Protestant. Try to blend in. Some will move north, and West. I guess these Masipkoi will head back to Odanak, when the war is over, and Canada belongs to the British."

"That is a horrible thought, my brother."

"Well, maybe they'll be kinder than the Bostonians. Couldn't be much worse. I guess a lot of the French will stay. Maybe we should move up there."

"What about the woods? The Koasek intervales?"

"That might answer for a while. But they'll take the *koasak abaziak* just like they took the great meadow, our old home. The lower Koas will be British settlements within a few months, you can bet on that. I would bet money those ancient glades will be a huge, open field in a generation's time. Grandfather saw their axes on those trees in a vision—the machines they will make someday."

"God, they're evil." Gihla's eyes looked hollow, imagining British men felling the massive, ancient *koasak*, killing the spirits who filled her family's beloved meadow with such vibrant power. "I cannot imagine how such a sin would weigh on their soul. Begwedzo will visit them in their sleep, or when they die, and make them sorry. He will ruin the rivers, the forests, the great Bitawbákw, the earth and sky. They will see."

She lay down and closed her eyes, and soon, she entered a dream state. Effortlessly, she traveled astrally to her first family, so many years before, the morning after. Age brought closeness to the spirit realm...young children, and old people dwelt closer to the streams of connection with other worlds. Memories offered themselves up to her. Her mind set images before her, her mother's memories, near sixty years gone. She could see her own experience, but now she could see more. Her mother and father's courtship, her own conception—her family, storytelling at the Ktsi Pôntekw during the fishing season. She watched the images in her head like a moving picture, playing complex family history in her dreams.

1692

In Gihla's vision, bright light streamed generously on the pair, sunning on the rocks. Ten winters had passed since this young girl was taken from her British parents, and she'd gone fully native. A river of green, glassy water poured through a carved, white granite streambed, and her senses were alive. The family had migrated, feeling crowded at Schaghticoke after Sadochquis and other northern Alnôbak moved in. Still defiant, unwilling to move so far from their ancestral homes, they resisted the move so many others had made north to Canada. They left and headed west, over two mountain ridges and into wooded Sokwaki territory north of Sokwakheag, where so much devastation had taken place in the last three generations. Currently there was an English settlement there, the northernmost one on the Kwanitekw, the long river. But they were ten leagues north of that, and felt reasonably safe. Besides, it made a good place to strike from. Wawanolewat had traveled quite a bit on different wartime errands, and some of the fleetest men from the small group traveled with him. Just four years before, he raided Deerfield with a band of angry Sokwakiak, who rebelled when the French tried to make them move up into Quebec. They even burned French villages, on the way south. Now they were back in the Sokwakiak homeland, at least for a while.

And here, now, Gihla beheld a beautiful place, a holy place. Impeccably clean, round rocks sat at the edge of the river in stone depressions carved over hundreds of years. A spreading waterfall brought the water down in stages, majestically, to a wide river basin. Generations upon generations of Nebilinto's ancestors had come here, and stories of the place echoed deep in the collective Alnôbak memory. The Ktsi Pôntekw.

There was another such place just south of Sokwakiak, and still another to the southeast—but Bostonians had moved in everywhere since Turner's massacre of helpless dawnlanders during Metacom's final year. These colonists sold plenty of alcohol, but wouldn't part with guns or ammunition; they dammed rivers, cut and burned every tree, let the brush grow without burning it; continually damaging, bespoiling, wreaking havoc on the land. For personal gain, some renegade Sokwakiak had sold some of the former homeland to them. This action, though unthinkable for many, had the side benefit of appeasing the invaders a bit, and (along with ongoing hostility) prevented further movement north. So north of Northfield, apart from an occasional explorer, the old territory held, and Bilinto, Zwame and their families enjoyed its wealth. They kept crops on the Ktsi Mskodak just south of the falls, and hunting was good in this area. But what they waited for now were fish.

Round, carved faces looked out at them from the rocks, everywhere it seemed, and Bilinto worked on one of his own in a lazy manner. Zwame had just woken from a nap. The world was awake, aware of their presence, and it filled their senses in return.

Bilinto ran his eyes over every inch of her bare skin. Noticing her perceptive smile, he made a pretense of concern. "You should cover yourself up. Your skin cannot take this sun." She remembered past sunburns, and knew he was right. She certainly wouldn't mind a bath in one of the natural tubs, to cool her body. She wandered off toward the cold, luxurious, scintillating water.

This was a place of light and power, it was easy to see. Hundreds of etched faces heightened the effects, staring wide-eyed from the water-carved, smooth white granite. The stream-bed revealed an endlessly fascinating sculpture, fashioned by centuries of dawnland engravers, and the force of water through the ravine. The round faces had round eyes and a mouth, and some had rays of energy coming from their heads. She knew there were large burial grounds just above the stream, on the west side of the river, and that this was a place of ancient power for Bilinto's people. She was nearly overwhelmed by her sense of place, and wondered what it must be like for him.

Maybe a hundred people were gathered along the rocky gorge, stacking baskets, looking around the base of the waterfall. From down below, excited people called up, "Here they come!" Everyone ran for a basket.

Long, silver shapes began to flash through the water, and leap from pool to pool as the people tried to catch them. The huge fish darted, sleek and beautiful, with soft fins, short mouths, and small, dark spots on their silver sides. *Mskwamagw,* a creature of great spirit-power. Wizwame could see their spirit-bodies leaping through the air. Many of them were huge, the length of her leg. Men laughed with pleasure as they flipped the biggest fish out of the main stream, and wrestled them in the smooth, granite basins of the riverbed. Baskets were handy for scooping and flinging fish on to the flat, rocky areas where people were ready to gather them. Racks were prepared for hanging and drying the meat, and many people began to cut the smooth, wet bodies open, to enjoy the savory meat within. People gave thanks, and so a two-week party began. Quick *wigwôms* sprang up throughout the woods, above and below the falls.

Gihla's dream was lucid, and she found herself able to view the landscape from any angle, and to assume any person's consciousness and perspective. Bilinto looked about eighteen, handsome in his breechclout, with his belt wrapped twice around his waist. He was strong and well coordinated, and had balanced judgment and a good sense of humor. Zwame had greatly enjoyed growing up with him, and nursed a crush on him for years until he finally proposed, just a month before, by sending her a wampum string through their friend Kowane. Needless to say, she kept it, indicating her acceptance. Since then they had slept head to foot, practicing partnership in the abstinent Alnôbak way. So far they seemed to live together easily. To show his betrothal, Nebilinto began to wear his hair braided and coiled on top of his head, held by a thong.

Many of the adolescents found Zwame's fair skin and hair very distracting, and she regarded them like so many sad, longing puppy dogs. Still, they were also happy for Bilinto, and, well, they had some other redeeming individual qualities. They could be annoying, but their attention was flattering as well. Zwame was not very tall, but well built, and the dawnland lifestyle and clothing—a breechclout and belt, and a knee-length skirt—allowed her the freedom to enjoy moving her body. She was now very grateful to have escaped the severe Pilgrim conditioning to cover up, and exhibit extreme discomfort at the sight of human skin. The memory of those days seemed painful. She wore thin deerskin shorts underneath the skirt, and her round breasts were covered with deerskin triangles tied in back and around her neck with narrow strips of leather, just to keep them under control.

Bilinto lifted a big salmon out of the river, holding it by its gills as it thrashed its tail in the water. He had a ring on his finger, which bore the letters IHS and a cross. It glinted in the sunlight—a present from an elder in his community. "Hey Zwame, this one's for you! I'll put it in your bed tonight!"

"You'll be cleaning and remaking my bed yourself while I sleep in yours! Here, throw that over here." She reached out her hands, and he heaved the fish neatly into a natural depression in the dry rock. She dispatched it with her hand axe, thanked it for giving its life, and brought it over to one of the people preparing the feast, a young man of twenty. He gave her a big smile, and spoke to her.

"Thanks! Your hair is so beautiful in this sunlight. It is hard to believe you're human, and not some strange goddess, with your golden hair like birch leaves in the fall. But I know you well enough."

"You are too kind, Bezoak. I'm glad your family could be here for this incredible wonder this year. The *mskwamagok* honor us, and we are lucky, lucky, blessed by the Spirit! This is my second year at this event, and I think it's my favorite time all year, even better than harvest. Do these fish really come from the ocean? I've never seen the ocean."

"Nor have I. But I have heard it stretches farther than you can see, so that the land seems small next to that big water. I don't know if it's true, that they come from the big water. But where else could they come from? They come here to safe water to lay their eggs. Where are your parents staying?"

"Wawanolewat has shelter and a sweat hut on the north end of the compound. Bilinto and I have a fire there. Which you must come visit later."

"I must come by, to honor your father, and to visit you! Will you stay and enjoy some of these sweet meats with me?"

"No, I want to get back and help Bilinto. He'll hit his head or something if I don't keep an eye on him." She wandered back, idly watching the people wading in the pools and snatching at the fish, or scooping with round baskets and pulling up large silver missiles, flashing and wriggling in the sun. Bilinto was too appealing to resist, his body glistening with river water, positive energy streaming out of him like sunlight. He was delighted, and it showed. She tackled him into a sandy pool, and wrestled him in the shallows.

"Oh, I'm sorry! I thought you were a fish. You look like one." She grinned at him, though he was now holding her down against a smooth, wet rock. Their feet were in the shallows.

He laughed. "You better watch yourself. Some of these fish are too big for you to play with. They might get the better of you."

"I'd give it a try." She tried a quick move on him, and almost pulled him over. She did manage to pull away, and crouched, pretending she would spring again. He looked relaxed, and she knew he would quickly defeat her if she tried. He was one of the better wrestlers in their little confederation. Still, she couldn't resist attacking him. She stood up suddenly, and walked over to a small boulder and sat down. "It's a beautiful day, isn't it?

"It's a blessing to be alive on a day like today."

"That's just what I was saying a few moments ago to Bezoak."

The two of them took a few quiet moments, simply to observe the scenery—the water, the sunlight, the rock, the people. The world waxed euphoric today, all day. The *omwaimenakwam* were in full bloom. Magic filled the air, and flashed in the water.

The silver, bony *wôbamagwsizak* massed in the shallows here too, flashing in abundance, but Wizwame saw none of the big, striped fish of Hoosac and Schaghticoke. During the first week, mayflies appeared for a day, hanging in midair with their three tails, and filling the sky as high as her eye could distinguish their tiny shapes. The river frothed with leaping *mowômagok*, eating hatching insects. Big *wadamobamegwezidak* ranged along the shore, beating fish into rocky shallows with their massive paws, or tossing them from their teeth. *Megezoak* and *maanamagwasak* circled, and two *ceskwadadasak* kept busy, darting and diving from bushes by the riverside. The inhabitants of the world, it seemed, were feasting.

Gihla's dream moved ahead, to a new scene. On the seventh night, the drum circles and the dancing began. *Namaskan Kizos*, the fishes' moon, hung clear and full in the sky. The men and the women separately painted and dressed themselves in their finest clothing, and danced for fun, giving thanks for their abundant blessings. They feasted and talked. The Sokwakiak honored the spirits of their ancestral dead, buried just across the river. In adult gatherings, they also remembered their sorrows—including the thousands who had died just two generations ago of small-pox in Sokwakiak, where almost no one survived.

A generation after that, some elders remembered, saw the slaughter of their people in a fierce battle with the Kanienkehaga, who arrived with four hundred warriors, and used a hundred in a suicide mission to draw out the Sokwakiak warriors; thinking they were chasing the remnants of a failed invasion, the men streamed from their palisaded village of Fort Hill directly into the teeth of three hundred Kanienkehaga warriors hidden behind a knoll, who in turn overran the village and killed all but about twenty hidden survivors. In their attempt to resist the historic Maqua tribute levied on the Mohican, Pocumtuck, and Sokwakiak, they were vanquished. So it was, the Sokwakiak experienced the destruction of Fort Hill, their last ancestral home.

Some remembered times the Alnôbak repaid the Kanienkehaga over the next generation. Other family bands remembered personal sorrows; two families of Penacooks had their story of woe. Wawanolewat told some of his own war stories, recounting the death of Woronokes, Pocumtucks and other eastern Indians at Sheffield in 1675, as they were chased by Massachusetts soldiers on the way to Schaghticoke. Then, he launched into some of his legendary stories of creeping around settlements, causing terror. The dawnland people laughed as he told of slipping latches and leaving doors open at night—of letting livestock silently out into the road—of gathering pies and bread from windowsills—of jumping out of the forest, making faces at housewives, and laughing as they screamed, amid their laundry piles and billowing sheets.

The family now numbered eleven; Alita remarried and moved north with Abesani. Atahla had a new daughter, named Wanlina, now three. Oladaka died of measles, and afterward Jajigwiwi took five Kanienkehaga arrows in the torso, fighting Massachusetts English from Fort Wilderness alongside Mohicans, just before the group left Schaghticoke. He died a few hours later. Seated with a group of prominent warriors at the falls, Malalemet told the story of his last few days.

"We breached the palisade, and came up against the door to the fort, my brother and I, Ariskantak and Begoag. Covered by our bowmen at the south and west end, we started in with hatchets. An Hodinohso:ni war party came from the north, and caught us in a deadly crossfire. Jajigwiwi took two shafts in the ribs—I heard him gasp, and looked up at him—he stared into the eyes of death. He looked at the Kanienkehaga, and turned to face them, so his full, standing body could protect ours. His left hand gestured, once, for us to run, even as he took another arrow. This all happened within seconds, I think, though time was very strange, as I reeled in horror. I yelled out, and our warriors ran around to engage the enemy. Then I was angry, and set to hacking at the door, as my brother remained standing. Two more arrows, and he sank to his knees. I looked, and the Hodinohso:ni were beating us back to the entrance. I turned Jajigwiwi around. I gripped his arms, and looked him in the eye. He met my gaze, closed his eyes, and fell. I could see I'd be dead if I stayed. We ran—slipped through the gate just as we lost control. We broke for the woods, and many of us made it out alive."

Wawanolewat said, "Your memory shows his bravery. Your choice to live, your intelligence. I am deeply glad of it. We will sing for Jajigwiwi. We mourn his loss."

They honored the memory of Metacom; though many

Alnôbak had blamed him for starting the conflagration that gave the now numerous British an excuse to massacre indiscriminately, they recognized the real error belonged to his father, Massasoit, who foolishly pitied the miserable, starving English, and allowed them to stay in the dawnlands, not realizing they'd soon arrive by the thousands in those huge, wooden ships, packing explosive weapons. Many there attended the great war conferences at Schaghticoke, back when they still hoped to drive the British back to their ships. Soon after that, the white men began to show their true colours once again. An old Pocumtuck told about finding the bodies at the Ktsi Pôntekw south of Sokwakiak, the day after that massacre during the last year of Metacom's war, and everyone understood—fierce resistance offered the only hope, the only possible strategy against such people, and they needed to stifle pity and mercy now to survive.

"Women and children lay dead in their broken *wigwôms*. Many had clothes ripped off. We dragged and buried over seventy people." The British now called this Turners Falls, in honor of the butcher we killed there, too late, after he ordered his Englishmen to murder unprotected old men, women and children who gathered for the spring fish harvest. Others recounted raids two years ago at Brookfield where they lost fourteen men after many successes; and last year at Deerfield, where they killed eight in the springtime, and abducted a man in the fall, sending him north to Mazipskoiodanak. We successfully drove a few colonists from our homeland in Sokwakiak—the English call it Northfield now. They ran from their farmhouses into the night. We burned everything. If they have nothing, maybe they will stay to the south and east."

Toward the end of that conflict, the British caught, killed, dishonored, and dismembered Metacom, and placed his head on display on a pole. No Indian would soon forget that grotesque statement of British dominance.

Gihla watched as Zwame moved freely from one age group to another, and after listening to the men's warlike discussion for a while, she visited the women, who had left as the talk turned violent to gather, clean and fillet the fish, and prepare it for smoking. The smokers were going all night—women cut wood, and tended the fire—the men had dug the long tunnels through the bank, with a chimney at the far end, and the women simply put the fish on racks in the middle, started a fire at the lower end, and kept it smouldering. They were able to preserve a huge amount of food in this way, which usually lasted to midwinter.

She listened to their talk, laughed with them, and wandered into a long house where children were gathered, listening to an older man telling Sokwakiak and Mazipskoiak stories of Ktsi Nwaskw, who created the Alnôbak from living wood; of the hero Bedegwadzo, a good and powerful spirit who could control weather; of Pmola, a flying creature with an *megezo* head, possessed of great power, and very dangerous; of Manógemassak, the thin-headed, tiny people living at the bottom of lakes and streams, who crafted buildings and dugout canoes of stone and paddled away quickly into deeper water, when they heard humans coming. Then there were endless silly stories of the raccoon Azeban, who fooled people until she was undone by her own scheming.

Zwame listened until she grew as sleepy as the small children, who were beginning to march off to their beds. She finally caught up with Mejejaawi, listening to Wawanolewat addressing the men, talking about the threats of King William against the "renegade" Alnôbak peoples. Wawanolewat finished in his clear and powerful voice: "We stand strong against the Bostonnais. We said that. We want it that way."

Malalemet—the tall, stern man with the scarred arm who'd abducted her as a child, Wawanolewat's brother—began to relate yet another recent horror story.

"Hear what I have to say. Just a few months ago, in the dead of winter, I was up at Mazipskoiodana and joined an army of six hundred French, Kahnawake Kanienkehaga and Alnôbak heading south across Bitawbákw, the lake between the Alnôbak and Kanienkehaga people, to strike at Albany and the British forces of Governor Slaughter and Major Peter Schuyler. The governor had recently moved all the remaining Schaghticokes to Half Moon at the mouth of the Kanienkehaga River, forcing them to serve his military interests, and causing great resentment among the River Indians.

Our force was successful in its march to the region, and easily took three castles just above Schenectady. We killed or captured over three hundred people, sustaining few losses. Soon, however, over two hundred of Schuyler's regiments joined with over a hundred Kanienkehaga, and engaged our army north of Albany, with severe loss on both sides. We captured over fifty Kanienkehaga, and began to close ranks and back away from the battlefield. Right then, eighty more British regulars appeared at their left flank, under Captain Syms, and things would have been disastrous if a snowstorm hadn't come up, and covered our retreat. Still, many good men had been lost or frozen in the storm, and exposure took a heavy toll on the three hundred or so of us still remaining. The following morning we kept up our march as quickly as they could, but Schuyler's men, who had better shelter and woolen clothing, caught up to us and retook the Kanienkehagak prisoners, neatly cutting them out of our retreating body.

They made to attack and decimate us all, but an amazing phenomenon saved over two hundred men; a bridge of ice stretched across the heaving Muheannaheanock held us as we sprinted as light as we could, in single file. It finally broke up before the last fifty men could make it across, and twenty or more fell into the freezing river—almost all were lost forever. But those who made it across were safe from the threat of the forces allied against them, on the opposite shore. But now we had to make it home, and the weather turned even colder. Starving men ate their pouches, their shoes, and in final desperation, even the corpses of men who died on the trail, along the shores of Bitawbágók.

I broke off with twelve men and headed up the Onegígwizibó, crossing the ancient passes to Mkazawitekw, which as you know enters the Kwanitekw right here, just above the Ktsi Pôntekw, making the big *bakwaaskwol* marsh where we will hunt *gwigwigwemok* and *wôbtegwak* tomorrow, if you will join me." He smiled at a few of the teenagers, who were visibly excited at the prospect of this excursion. Then he continued his story.

"Our woodcraft and successful hunting allowed us safe passage, but we feared widespread losses among the larger force headed to Canada, and we were right; close to half the army perished on the winter traverse, and the remainder had arrived, starving, merely a sixth of their original numbers. Still, the French counted it a successful strike, and said we put fear of French and Alnôbak strength across the wooded, northern reaches of British territory."

As the men reflected, it burned in dawnland hearts that the lower control of the rivers remained clearly in British control, and they realized the colonists to the south also enjoyed the *mskwamagok*, no doubt netting it along the entrance to the river, where it met the wide ocean. Still, clearly, many of the fish made it through to the brooks where they'd hatched, to enjoy the springtime process of love and renewal.

Gihla watched her mother walk out of one of the groves of nut trees that filled the lowlands on this stretch of the river valley. The trees cast distinct shadows into the bath of moonlight by the edge of the river. She looked up along the shore, and she saw Nebilinto had followed her out, and now stood watching her, and smiling. She walked up to him and they embraced, slow, and put their mouths together. Time seemed precious, and he was so beautiful, and they had known and loved each other so long. They made their own little camp, and spent their first full night in each other's arms.

In the morning, their love was known among their families simply by looking at them, and everyone was happy with the budding young love in this beautiful place, where spirits were so full, and this sort of thing was to be expected. People smiled and passed knowing looks, and a bit of light seemed to shimmer off the two lovers as they went about their morning activities, and headed for the falls where everyone gathered for another beautiful day.

The youths wandered to the base of the falls, and began to walk in their patterned, laced *mozak* skin moccasins along the wooded western shore, laughing and chasing each other along old paths. They continued in this way, running with the speed of young Alnôbak, with sunlight streaming, and birds singing and flitting through the trees. They followed the river, and stopped to drink at clean sections of stream along the way, helped each other over rocks and up embankments, and stopped to view the land from a ridge about a half a league south of the falls.

They could see the turn of the river toward the falls, and the tall *koasak abaziak*, the pines of their camp, on the high, eastern end of the falls. To the south, another stand of massive *koasak,* even taller and older, stood on a generous floodplain on the west side, which bulged into a sweeping bend in the river. Some of the land lay open and grassy, and from where they were they could see birds and a large *moz*, grazing along a meadow's edge, by low trees which swept upward into a massive, dark glade of *koasak*. Drawn by invitation from the majestic trees, they walked down the hill and across the meadows, which had straggling, colored *skamonal* volunteering with the *sagadaboak, bakwaaskwol* and *môlôgwimenal.* They crossed through the brushy edge of the meadow, disturbing *mikoak* and a *bakeso,* fluttering loudly away through the understory, as they made their way along a narrow path. The brush hadn't been burned in many years, and needed clearing. Still, the canopy kept the growth low, and the experience of wandering into these tall *koasak*, with shafts of yellow light spiking through tall, ancient growth, felt like entering the home of powerful wood spirits, or angels.

They separated for a while, to enjoy the feeling of walking alone in the magnificent grove. Though the midday sun was out, and an occasional knife of sunlight penetrated the white and yellow pines, it was generally dark and hushed on the forest floor, as if it that bit of earth had only known dusk and nighttime for hundreds of years. Forest animals made their homes there, and walking silently, Zwame was able to observe many of them. Woodfowl fluttered, abundant along the forest floor, and she could hear a variety of songbirds, and see them nesting in the thick pine branches. The grounds were mostly soft and thick with brown needles.

Last year saw huge cone growth, and piles of green and brown cones lay strewn among the needles and branches. The *masozi* reached well past the fiddlehead stage, and along with patches of huge, ancient *odamôganizak, dkinoganizal* and the spicy *skogadebakwol* ranged around. In general, there were a lot of foodstuffs. She dug up numerous bulbs, and put them in the leather satchel she always carried at her side with its flint knife. She was digging with the knife in a large patch of ancient, flowing *dzidziwol pes-kwasawônal*—huge purple, three-leaved woodland beauties—when she heard cracking branches behind her. She turned and looked through the trees, and was startled to see two white colonists in thin, grey woolen clothes, walking through the brush toward her. They had seen her. The warm cloth of serenity seemed rent in two.

Wizwame jumped up, held her knife at the ready, and gave the 'urgent' whistle for Nebilinto. He came bounding through the woods toward her, arriving at the same time as the white men walked up to the girl. The pairs stood facing each other—tension in the air, but no distinctly threatening gestures. One of the colonists looked thick-set with a brown beard. The other was wiry, showing more age, and a few days of stubble. Zwame watched the older man take in Bilinto's ring. The bearded one spoke.

"You're a white girl? "A Christian?" The sound of English was always a little strange to her after these many years, though not completely unfamiliar. She heard some words among her people, at times, and had been witness to soldiers and traders discoursing with some of her group, particularly Wawanolewat and Mejejaawi. Also, she had spoken in English with Mejejaawi frequently when she was young, and occasionally in past years. So she did understand it well enough.

"No, no more. I am Woronoke. This young man is Sokwaki. This is his homeland. Why are you here?"

"We wanted to see what the land was like north of where we live. We're from Northfield. My name's Tom Wells, and this is my friend Benoni Stebbins. These are beautiful pines."

"Yes, they are ancient, and should be respected." They stood for a moment, listening to the forest.

"Where are you from? Do you know who your parents are?" The words tumbled out of the bearded man, and he looked her in the eye.

She paused a moment before speaking. "I lived in Westfield, a long time ago. My name was Sackett." She felt resolute, not wanting to see her birth family, but could not keep down flickers of wonder and longing.

"There is a Sackett who came up to Northhampton some years ago, lost a daughter many years back from Westfield. I expect that is you."

"John Sackett?"

"Yes, that's his name. We'll tell him you are alive."

"Don't. It would only cause trouble."

"Seems a man's got a right to know."

A long pause followed. Finally Zwame said, "You shouldn't be here. You shouldn't have come up here. We would kill you if you came further up river."

"Thanks for the warning. I think we'll head back south. We wouldn't want to bite off more n' we can chew," the bearded man said, smiling. The other seemed impassive. "Be seein' ya around."

"Not a good idea."

The bearded man held up his hand for farewell, and the pair started walking south through the woods, to where they probably had a canoe downriver. Bilinto and Zwame stood watching. When the men left their sight they quickly circled around to the riverbank above them, and slowly crept along through narrow paths in the brush until they spotted the men pushing out in their native-built canoe, paddling south. They kept heading downriver.

"We should get back up to the falls and share this news." The pair headed at a quick pace back up the river, past *benegôkihla-sizak* that dived from little holes in the riverbank, and swooped in dizzying spirals over the surface of the water, catching insects. Along the way, large fish leapt and splashed, and birds called to each other. Zwame was preoccupied, though, even more than Bilinto, as they made their return trip.

Upon reaching home they told the elders in their households, and the word quickly spread, though there was no panic. The colonists had not seemed to be any organized group, and were more interested in Zwame than in their camps and positions. Wawanolewat and Mejejaawi took particular interest in the discussion about the Sackett family in Northhampton. They questioned the girl, each at different times over the next two days, about her feelings, and intentions. She said to each that she had learned to love them as family, forever, and her old family was dead to her. But they could tell it was not the entire truth.

A new scene appeared in the dream. Mejejaawi taught Wizwame simple birth control methods, using timing of menstruation as a general rule, and a *pehanem* root rinse. She kept giving her advice, until Zwame finally said, "Aunt, they should have named you Begwiojaawi, you keep picking at me so much!" Everyone laughed at the pun, a reference to the tiny, annoying midges that made it through every opening in a blanket to nip at you.

But really, Zwame was grateful. The women encouraged her not to enjoy Bilinto too much until she felt ready to care for children. She was still young, having just come of age the year before, and they didn't want her to rush into anything. She saw they were wise and mostly heeded their advice, and Bilinto proved entirely respectful of her wishes. He would wait for a woman he loved so much, and he was lucky that he didn't always have to.

Zooming along in her astral travels, months flashed through Gihla's consciousness. Summer grew out of the celebration, and foods were plentiful, especially the luscious, pink *mskwamagok* meat for weeks afterward, and leafy greens, the spicy *skogadebakwol*, and succulent *minobowigek peskwasawônal*. Skies remained clear and beautiful, though powerful, intimidating thunderstorms came at times, with cool air sweeping in during and after, relieving the thick haze of humidity. Evenings were wonderful. The summer swept on, and a blissful, dry autumn came, and winter after that. Following Nebilinto's wishes, they didn't go far—they just moved south to the great pine meadows, following a stream up into the hills a little, and building homes there. It seemed an easy place to be, with little threat from the south at this point.

Military actions were few, and mostly seemed far away—though French mounted a small attack on Deerfield again that year, Frontenac was more concerned with attacking Kanienkehaga and Yorker British again from the north, and continually organized people from Masipskoiodanak, and made plans to send them with his own troops down into Oneida and Onondaga land, on the offensive. Wawanolewat kept good contacts with his brother and other friends to the north. True, the previous year a group of untrustworthy Algonkians came from Albany, and the suspicious Sokwakiak and their small confederation argued until a fight broke out between them. This was settled more in the old Indian way, with threats and only a few blows; the strangers were run off, and did not come back that year.

So Zwame and Bilinto were comforted; the current battleground stayed blissfully far away from the Sokwakiak homelands, and things remained peaceful in the cathedral pines, the massive stand of *koasak*. Near the forest, a beautiful brook rolled down from low mountains, and they followed it up into a range of low, rolling hills. Along the streambed, in one location, they found a carved stone face, clearly very old. The family decided it was there to welcome them, and might offer powerful protection.

Further up, along one stretch of ridge to the southwest, her family came across two ancient stone rooms set into the earth, with unusual markings on the walls and the floor. Mejejaawi thought that they might have been made by early Europeans passing through, hundreds of years earlier, when trade routes flourished throughout the continent—before anyone had heard of smallpox, diphtheria, dysentery, scarlet fever, measles, typhoid, alcohol, property, and endless other evils. She had heard of such white people, traveling far, before any large ships existed. The ancient memory of these men came to her through her mother, who told her they were wise and friendly, unlike anyone who came across the great waters now. Wawanolewat disagreed. For him, the chambers were Indian, made by ancient Sokwaki masons.

Zwame and Bilinto sometimes slept in one set high up on a hillside, with three-foot stone walls propping a low, stone ceiling. It had a groove carved into the doorway for drainage—when it rained, a bowl of water formed, which emptied out the front without bothering the couple inside, dry and warm between their furs. They loved the pattering sound, and the fresh air. When they awoke, there was a place to drink, and wash their faces.

Another room, a more elaborate, five-foot diameter circular foundation covered by a stone and dirt roof, nested in the floor of a hardwood glade. It made a fabulous root cellar. They could put by enough grain and other foods for a long winter.

The best room of all yawned further down in the valley, just a league north of the round cellar hole. This massive stone structure had huge slabs making up the roof and lintel, and dirt mounded around and above. Five could sleep comfortably, and so they made this spot the primary settlement for the winter and set up two domed *wigwôms* nearby. Wawanolewat dowsed the chambers with hickory twigs, and found water crossings at every stone chamber site, without exception.

Thus they made their homes both in and above ground—in the summer, the rock rooms were cooler, and in winter, given a few hot, granite streamstones, much warmer than the exposed *wigwôms*. They kept a family *wigwôm* above ground for most of the people, with its multiple rooms and fires for each nuclear family. During this time, she and Bilinto set up their own room, adding a fourth to the line of campfires seen as she looked from one end of the long house to the other. In the fall, the first year, they burned out the underbrush, and afterward harvests and hunting were excellent just a mile down the brook. She and Bilinto lived a blissful life despite the constant threat of British soldiers, who never discovered or disturbed the family during this period of their lives.

Still, another two years passed before she felt ready to have a child, and soon after she and Bilinto made their decision. Despite occasional differences and arguments their love had not faded in the least, and they knew all along it was a matter of time if nothing else came in their way. During her pregnancy Zwame was excited and happy, and also tired, sick, and scared, at times, but she held herself with the dignity of a Wôbanaki woman, showing little of it. For their parts, the elder women of her household treated her regally. They carried endless knowledge of herbs and foods, and treated her to nettle and oatstraw teas, oil rubs, and more food than she really wanted, to tell the truth. Generally, she basked in the attentions she received from her family, and not least from Bilinto.

They worked hard in the face of the many challenges life brought daily, and field and other manual labor continued for Zwame right up until the day her child was born. She had conceived in midwinter, and brought it right through to term at harvest as if she had a *wasawa* growing inside her. It lasted a little longer, and grew a little larger than *wasawa* in the field, as frost could not affect her child and she tended it well, eating well and staying healthy. She was cutting small wood and breaking kindling when she felt the wetness on her leg, and knew her time had begun. A few hours later, on a clean mat on the forest floor near the rushing brook, her labor was steady.

With the help of the three women, she held off until they could feel the child's head pushing her open wide. Her strong effort followed—an incredible experience, with tears and strong words, and lights appearing in her head when she closed her eyes—and out came a child, with light brown hair, browner skin, and dark brown eyes. At first the eyes appeared frustrated, shocked by the light and air, then later wide with wonder as the child tasted colustrum and milk. It was hard to get him to latch on at first, and Mejejaawi was happy to help her hold his head. Wizwame lost herself in those eyes for days afterward, nursing and cuddling with the child, and the hugely proud Bilinto.

The child's skin was lighter than his, which didn't bother the parents, but made them remember the English heritage. They called him Kazawinamito. Black eyes. He nursed well and grew quickly, and brought joy to the entire family through the cold winter that followed.

Gihla opened her eyes, and gazed at the walls of her *wigwôm* with a deep understanding.

1763

Daniel Sackett came through his doorway in the bright light of morning. The fields rippled with the new wheat, and his three heifers lowed for mash and milking, which his grandchildren would get to before long. Home was a comfort to him.

Three years had passed since he'd read the posted flyers about Rogers' grueling march north up the Champlain valley and west of Montreal to St. Francis, to put an end to the raids and killing that characterized a hundred years of settlement in the Massachussetts colony. They had raided the Indian village in the morning, leaving only a few children alive. Not a nice memory, according to a Ranger Sackett spoke to at the Landlord Fowler Tavern, a man named Martin Severance. The man had a lot of stories, including a time he'd been taken prisoner in 1757.

Severance said Rogers drove his men like animals, and when they finally attacked, they acted like animals, spearing heads on their muskets and cutting ears for trophies. The return trip was a killer—lost, they fled south from the French and Indians, then roamed through brutal winter to the Connecticut. Starving, they butchered prisoners and ate them. Well upriver they spooked their resupply detachment, which in turn fled south, fearing they were Indians, leaving them nothing. Many died, or lost toes from frostbite. In the end, they came into Fort Number Four nearly dead. It took two weeks there to nurse the men back to life, and send them down river on the final trip home.

Back home in Deerfield, Severance said, he was greeted as a hero. The New England papers reported Rogers' men killing two hundred people, and torching the entire town. It seemed a final punctuation mark on the years of war—immediately after,

France finally gave in, and England had taken all the territory north and west of Massachussetts. Where once the land had terrified them, colonists flocked in droves. The town populations north of Deerfield quickly tripled, and quadrupled. Daniel, now seventy and set in his ways, had no desire to pull up and move off, and neither had his nine remaining children. They had a small village of their own up on the ridge now, with Sackett family farms, including his daughters' families, the Williamses and the Comstocks, ranging a full two and a half miles up the road.

Daniel finished the milking, and came out the barn carrying pails to the house. Looking up, his attention was drawn by something unusual.

A lone man straggled down Sackett Ridge Road, wearing a white linen shirt and blue cotton trousers, looking old and strong, and not a little out of place. Daniel could see his chiseled native features, though his soft, trimmed grey hair showed some European blood. He drew near, and looked toward the old farmer.

"You a Sackett? Daniel Sackett?"

"I'll allow I am." Daniel paused a moment as they looked one another up and down. He knew about Elizabeth, and took a guess. "You a relative or something?"

"Yep. The English call me Sackett, actually. Your aunt was my mother."

"Elizabeth."

"Yes." A long pause. Their eyes met.

"Well, I guess you'd better come in." Daniel pushed open the door with his foot, and held it a moment for his nephew. He placed the pails on a table inside and pulled out a square of clean linen to strain the milk.

Saksis sat down at the wooden table, and stared at a loaf of bread that sat upon it. He drew a heavy sigh. A long silence passed. He spoke.

"I guess you've won now."

"Come again?" Daniel couldn't follow.

"The English. You've taken over. Moving in throughout the Wôbanaki territory. Hundreds of people. Thousands of people, cutting down the trees."

"That. Well, I guess so." Daniel poured two mugs of milk and set them down on the table. What did this man want, coming here?

"I wonder if you were a warrior, too." The man considered Daniel, seeing military service in his bearing, in his eyes.

"Yes, I served as a young man under Adgat Dewey, on a troop of horse, as a sentinel, when your grandfather raided our Connecticut river towns. I guarded Westfield under Hezekiah Noble and John Ashley. Many of my sons are soldiers, and farmers."

"I was a soldier, too."

Daniel's eyes showed a little fire. "I heard of you. You were a damn thorn through the seven years war. They made fun of me 'cause I'm a Sackett. Said I was on your side." He smiled at the memory. "A lot of people around here said Dad was always soft on the Indians."

The halfbreed grinned, a little sheepishly. "Yeah—I guess that could be a problem. No one called me a Pilgrim, though, except the prisoners in Chambly, when I was little. My men didn't make fun of me."

"I guess that's a benefit of leadership. My men won't let it go with my boys, and they still bring it up, when they come round to visit. Which, my boys might not be so glad to see you here."

"I'm not afraid of them. But I don't want to offend them either."

"Well, we've seen the outcome now. Like you said, we won. It'll all be English pasture in fifty years."

Saksis looked down. "That's a painful thought, to me."

"I can't help that." Daniel tried, but he couldn't sympathize. He thought of his father's early years—losing his barn, his daughter. He thought of his years riding scared on the lonely frontiers. He remembered dead comrades, deadly conflicts. What did this man want? No harm in asking.

"What can I do for you, anyway?"

"I just wanted to see someone. Someone from my mother's family." He looked around at the walls. He seemed satisfied, just to be allowed in the house. "I wanted a last connection. Now my people will roam—pulling up again, heading west. I'll probably stay in Quebec, finishing out my years hunting on land that isn't taken yet. I won't live very long, and I have no children. Like you, I grow old."

Another pause, then Daniel spoke. "We have our memories. Some are painful, but for our family, most are before our time. I can forgive what your family did to me. Can you forgive my people?" Despite his colonial stance, Daniel showed surprising awareness of the situation of the dawnland people—now killed, uprooted, dead of disease, unwelcome in all their old territories. The Sacketts were clearly not the most insensitive of families. Still, a wide gulf ranged between them. The elderly Daniel, in his Christian way, would bridge it if he could. But his strange cousin Sackett couldn't come across to meet him.

"I think not. That is too great a burden of guilt to wash away. But I can forgive one man at a time, maybe. I can forgive you." Sackett suddenly got a little misty at the eyes, and began to speak slowly. "This was my grandfather's land, right here. The circle of his fire. When he was a child, his family lived here in Tomhaumucke. Part of Woronoco. That child—the man who took your aunt—took back a family member, since so many had been taken from him. My people died in huge numbers, and what was once our brave land is no more. Our ways are lost. Maybe our language will be lost. Total destruction."

Reflecting, Daniel realized, the man did not overstate. He imagined life for the remaining Abenaki, the people of Missisquoi. He couldn't picture them sticking around when the charter holders took over, and the colonists came sweeping in. "That's the way of war, I guess. I wish we could have been more friendly to each other."

"The way of war for your people. Colonize, separate, destroy. Build fences. Square by square, corner by corner, you push until it belongs to you, and you only. The old trees, the animals are dying out. Fences and cattle. Fires and dams. A strange world you build." He stood to go.

Looking at it from this Sackett's perspective, he could not gainsay the man. But then, Daniel and his family were on the winning side, and these were good arguments to lose, as they couldn't affect the heavily weighted scale of power.

He shook hands with his cousin, showing the good faith of family, and watched him disappear into the woods. As he walked into his cottage, the thought stuck in his head: *Tomhaumucke.* The original name.

He sat at his table, cut a slice of bread, spread his butter, and chewed in silence.

Afterword &
Acknowledgements

The idea and inspiration for this novel came about during my family's early years in Putney. Sacketts Brook rolls past my house, continues two miles down to the village, passes over the dam by the Putney General Store, then crosses under the Calvin Coolidge Highway and tumbles past the recycled paper mill down to the Connecticut River. Putney is a beautiful Vermont town with a complex history of Perfectionists, industry, apple orchards and nurseries, schools, politics and protest. What the land was like before settlement is largely left to imagination, though we read in our first town history (1953) that massive white and yellow pines (*koasak*, in this book) loomed on the Ktsi Mskodak (Great Meadow), so great and majestic it was dark on the open, spacious forest floor in the daytime. No one at the historical society knew where the brook got its name, though a very few had heard of Sackett in other contexts, and these folks speculated a bit.

As an undergraduate advisee of historian Larry Hauptman at SUNY New Paltz, I knew a little about the Indians of the eastern woodlands, and I'd perused Haviland and Powers' *The Original Vermonters* and Colin Calloway's *The Western Abenaki of Vermont* repeatedly. Online, I found a tantalizing bit from *Woronoco: The History of Westfield* (p.3):

The records show that Elizabeth Sackett died on June 15, 1682, but long research proves this was false. Elizabeth was actually captured by Indians during a raid, other members of the family managing to get safely into the log house. Rev. E. Davis, in a history of this area, mentions the fact that the Indians captured a daughter of John Sackett and took her to northern New York.

Here she was raised as an Indian. Later, around 1710, Elizabeth visited Westfield with her Indian husband and son and daughter. As they were not used to living in a log house, they built a teepee where they lived while in Westfield. They eventually left and Elizabeth never returned, but her son grew up to be an Indian Chief and took his mother's name of Sackett. In later years Chief Sackett was well known around the area for his raids and he is mentioned by J.G. Holland in his *History of Western Massachusetts* as having attacked a detachment of soldiers near Heath, Massachusetts in 1748.

If only we could get a solid handle on the 'long research!' A 'teepee' is unlikely, as we are far from the Great Plains. One important reference is the account of a Doctor Davis, preserved in the Westfield Athaneaum, which states that "A daughter of the second wife of a Mr. Sackett (her name I do not know) was taken captive by the Indians and carried captive to the northwest part of New York, married an Indian and remained among them as long as she lived. Her descendants have been here to see their mother's friends several times since the French war. Previous to that they used some exertions to make others of the Sackett family captives but did not succeed." According to some accounts, the attack on Hobbs' men actually took place north of Heath, along the western trail from Fort Dummer, probably in the area of Marlboro, Vermont.

Years of archiving the Putney Historical Society's collection, and research for the 2003 history of Putney led me to numerous abduction stories like that of our first colonist, Nehemiah Howe, as well as Reverend Williams of Deerfield. I also discovered the Kathan family history (Col. Charles Kathan founded the Putney fort in 1753), which suggests that this particular Sackett had been the brook's namesake, without providing any specific evidence. No other Sacketts appear in any of our town's history, to my knowledge.

Mary Jane McGuire, librarian at Landmark College where I worked for many years, helped with interlibrary loan of a variety of primary and secondary source anthologies; these gave snippets of insight into events along the Connecticut from Deerfield to

Kowass, in central New Hampshire, and up in Mazipskoiodanak (a broad area ranging between the two settlements at what is now St. Albans, Vermont, and St. Francis, Quebec). While I did not make a careful listing of these, most can be found in the reference lists of Calloway's texts. I learned about Greylock's brother Malalemet, and the spread of disease and war; I began to form a big picture of the political tensions, and the changing landscape and economy. Claire Dacey of the PLACE project, whom I worked with in Putney in 2006, helped me to understand the geography, climate and the history of land use in southern Vermont, along with various authors including William Cronon and Tom Wessels.

Further online research brought a little more information about this amazing man Greylock, also known as Wawanolewat, who was first introduced to me by Colin Calloway. I am indebted to Google Books and Google Scholar for its remarkably useful catalog of pre-copyright texts, and to RootsWeb, as well as many Abenaki websites. Google Books offered the account of Susannah Johnson, among many other resources. Gordon Day's works taught me considerably more about Wawanolewat.

I traveled to Quebec, visiting various sites, and took in many sights locally along the Connecticut basin—petroglyphs, falls, islands, plants and animals, riverbank. I sailed and kayaked out of Burton Island, up by St. Albans, and hung around Burlington. I visited the Brooks Library in Brattleboro, Vermont. I researched at the Westfield archives, visited Sackett graves, and traipsed around the John Sackett homestead land, now riven by a railroad track. Many interesting people appeared during my summers at the Putney Historical Society, including dowser Leon Cooper, and Tod LaPlante from Northampton Mass, who along with our longtime Putney curator Laura Heller described the ancient, mysterious stone chambers scattered throughout the northeast (further discussed in the text Ancient Vermont), which figure in parts of this novel; debate continues as to their origins. I also worked closely with Addie Minott at the historical society in Guilford, Vermont, where I have taught middle school for many years, and tried to work in explanations for a mysterious few petroglyphs, such as the rocks showing the dates '1723' and '1745,' mentioned in the *Official History of Guilford*. Addie has shared the popular view that the rocks served as markers, and the petroglyphs on them point to significant, native waypoints.

Anthony Sheehan of Westminster, Vermont, an active Abenaki in the El Nu tribe, was helpful (members of his tribe, including his brother Mike, are on the cover of this book), and John Moody helped a great deal, both through taped lectures he'd given on Abenaki heritage in Putney in the early 1980s, as well as answering various questions I had late in the writing process. It was he who gave me the Abenaki name 'Saksis,' which I have used through much of the book. He explained that the name "Jacques Sachette," is also given for our title character by historical record, and that 'Sachette' translates to 'little Jacques' in French.

I am particularly indebted to Sackett family historian Thurmon King, whose advice and careful attention to details of the early Sackett family in America proved invaluable. Along with editorial suggestions, he explained that John Sackett's dam construction following the 1675 burning of his house and barn brought Pynchon court injunctions from his neighbors; he also noted allegations that Sackett traded with local, native groups in the early 1660's; he was nearly fined, but for lack of proof.

Late in the process, both Larry Hauptman and John Moody read my novel and offered invaluable feedback. John generously offered a linguistic and editorial review of the entire novel, and I attribute its current quality to his careful editing, without which this book would be a great deal less. It was interesting to note his linguistic differences with Gordon Day's dictionary, which often puts a 'g' where Abenakis would normally use a nice, hard 'k'.

I am very grateful to my wife, partner, and story editor, Julie Henry Strothman, a strong support all along, and the rest of my family, particularly my daughter Louisa who has shown interest in Elizabeth's story from the beginning, as well as my daughter Susanna and son Jacob, who have patiently listened to various historical musings along different parts of the Connecticut watershed. Susanna traveled with me to visit a number of stone chambers, and I have many happy memories of lowering her into ancient pits in the earth, which she seemed to enjoy immensely.

I am moreover very much indebted to Craig Brandon of Surry Cottage Books, a good friend and editor who helped in many ways, making it possible to finally bring this project to publication.

So what of this text is fiction, and what is fact? Truth is, I can have no idea how close or how far my guesses fall from the important marks in the story of Elizabeth and her son, Saksis. I still can't prove that Elizabeth Sackett was abducted, married native and had a child, or that the brook in Putney is named after her son. However, my research indicates these things are more than likely. A further reach is that Greylock abducted Elizabeth, and his family became hers; I can only say that Greylock was a Woronoke from Westfield, and reportedly raided heavily in that area as a young man as part of the ongoing insurgent skirmish with the colonists that took various forms of mischief, murder, property destruction, abduction, and inclusion of colonial children into the Algonquin communities. Therefore, he is a likely abductor. I can posit but not prove that along with the ailing Woronoke leader Soquans, Greylock lived at Schaghticoke, an important refugee center for western Massachusetts, where it is also rumored Elizabeth lived after her abduction. After moving to Schaghticoke, apparently many of the Woronokes split, some traveling north to join the Abenaki, others west to Mohican villages near Catskill, New York. Based on historical accounts, it is clear that Greylock, and consequently (in this story) Elizabeth Sackett moved north.

There is record of Greylock's compound near Mazipskoik later in life, as well as his various names, and the baptism of his child at Fort St. Frederic in the 1730s, when he must have been in his sixties at least. Malalemet appears in historical accounts, and there is some record of his work as a military leader and ambassador; the leaders and sachems I have named were mostly real people, as well as some random native characters such as Pinawans, and those variously associated with Brattleboro-area land sales, the Rogers raid on Odanak in 1759, or the garrisons at Fort Dummer and Fort Number Four. Many other dawnland people are my invention, including Nebilinto—I have no idea of his name or where he came from, and cannot prove he existed. Using Abenaki dictionaries from the magnificent scholar Gordon Day, whose works have been inexpressibly valuable in this process, I have also invented names for Wizwame, Namito, and most of Wawanolewat's extended family which I have no record of; Day's work has also informed my use of Abenaki words for plants and animals, and given the greatest detail in terms of native personalities, events, and population movements. My first glossary table was prepared by the public health scholar Anne H. Outwater using Gordon Day's lexicon. (Currently, Ms. Outwater is teaching nursing in Dar Es Salaam, Tanzania.) The final set of appendices was developed by John Moody, during his review of this novel.

The colonial history is more accessible, and as a result I can say that almost all the military events in this book happened, large and small (I can't think of any exceptions), and the "white" people mentioned in the story (including soldiers, traders, captives, and Catholic priests) did exist specifically by name and in the place where they appear in the story (though I did invent a few meetings such as that of Benoni Stebbins and Wizwame in the Putney Great Meadows, and some extra visits to the Sackett family in Westfield).

Within this historical context, the two events that tend to hit me hardest are the loss of the salmon, and the complete destruction of Sokwakiak, first by smallpox in the early 1630s, then by war in the 1660s. My understanding of these events is this:

Also known as Squakheag or Northfield, Massachusetts, the ancient Sokwaki village suffered a terrible epidemic of smallpox that killed about nine out of ten of its residents. The remaining people moved the village upriver, where it became known as Fort Hill, just below the present-day town of Vernon, Vermont. A few decades later it was utterly destroyed by visiting Mohawks, after a rash, unfortunate execution of their parley detachment by the Sokoki; in the end only a few residents survived, hiding in root cellars, or fleeing into the forest. This may be how the Mohawk Trail (Route 2 in northwest Mass.) got its name, though it is true that for centuries prior to the colonial period a large triangle of shared hunting ground existed, with its center at the "Salmon

Falls" in Shelburne Falls along Route 2 (due north of Westfield, where our protagonists originate).

And every spring as fishing season begins, I ponder the damming of the Connecticut River in 1799 in Turners Falls, which brutally blocked a large branch of Atlantic salmon, for good and all, from their ancient birthing grounds upstream.

The biological impact of this use of land for the purpose of industry is staggering. While I accept the need for economic development and the complexity of human history, I am at heart a Hudson River Sloop Clearwater guy, with many hours spent on Muheannaheanock (a Mohican name for the 'river that flows both ways'), catching fish in otter trawl nets and considering their migrations, and in summary I wish very much this bit of human accomplishment—all the big dams on the Connecticut, really—had never happened.

As for the postcolonial legacy, I would like everyone to accept that the Western Abenaki were definitely here in Vermont—and to think about our history, and our own actions right where we live, along the Kwanitekw watershed, and Bitawbákw, the lake between.

Finally, I will say that the impetus to write this novel came from Ella McDaid (speaker of the Northfield Mt. Hermon class of 2011), who having just moved from San Francisco, bravely declared at Guilford Central in 2006 that "November is novel writing month, and I'm going to write a novel."

That was crazy talk...and I couldn't let her go it alone.

Appendix A

Geographical Locations, Animal, Plant, and Other Names

In this book	Postcolonial (English)
Agaskwok	Woodchucks
Ahamoakezenal	Pitcher Plant
Alnizediak	Hemlock Trees
Alnôbak	The People (Original name of Abenaki)
Amiskw	Beaver (more commonly used for Pocumtuck areas)
Anaskaweziak	Red or Black Oak
Anaskaweziak Manhakwôgan	Red or Black Oak Inner Bark
Apenak	Ground Nuts (Plural)
Ashuelot	Ashuelot River, New Hampshire
Askaskwi Sibo	Green River, VT/Massachusetts
Asakwamal (Plural)	Moss
Awasosibemi	Bear Fat
Awasosak	Bears
Azeban	Racoon
Azebanak	Raccoons
Belazak (Plural)	Passenger Pigeons or Mourning Doves
Bagôn (Singular)	Butternut
Bagônal (Plural)	Butternuts
Bagônoziak	Butternut Trees
Bakesoak	Partridges

Bakwaaskol	Cattails
Bebonkiimadeqwasa	Northern Rabbit
Bebonkiimadeqwasak (Pl.)	Northern Rabbits
Begwiojawas	Sand Fly (No-See-Ums)
Benegôkihlasizak	Bank Swallows
Bitawbákw	Lake Champlain
Bitawbákok	At Lake Champlain
Bôbenôdagwezoak	Tamarack Trees
Ceskwadadasak	King Fishers
Temakwak (Plural)	Beaver
Dipwabel	Pepper
Dkinoganizal (Plural)	Jack-in-the-Pulpits
Dzidziwol peskwasawônal (Pl.)	Trillium Flowers (Purple)
Gagiwidahôzo	She is troubled, worried, or disturbed
Gogowibagwok (Pl.)	Wintergreen
Gwigwigemok (Pl.)	Ducks (General) or Black Ducks (Specific)
Kanibesinoak	Lower Kennebec River
Kanibesinoak Zibo	People of the lower Kennebec River
Kawazanamito	Black eyes
Kejegigihlasiz	Chickadees
Koa (Singular)	Pine Tree
Koasak (Plural)	Pine Trees
Koasak Abaziak	Pine Trees
Koasek (Place)/	Newbury, Vt & Haverhill, NH
Koasiak/Coosucks	(People)
Kokokhoakok	Balsam Firs
Ktsi Mskodak	Great Meadows of Putney, Vt
Ktsi Pôntekw	Bellows Falls, Vt/Walpole, NH (Great

	Falls)
Ktsi Niwaskw	Creator
Ktsitekw	St Lawrence River
Kwai	'Hello' in both Abenaki & Kanienkehaga
Kwanitegok	At the Connecticut River
Kwanitekw	Connecticut River
Kwezowahomak	Thompson's Point (Charlotte, VT)
Maanamagwasak	Ospreys
Magôliboak (Plural)	Caribou
Majimskikoal	Poison Ivy
Malomenal	Wheat
Manicknung	Stratton Mountain, Vt (possibly Mohican)
Menadenak	Stratton Mountain, Vt (Abenaki)
Maskwaiwigwaol	Birch Bark Canoe
Maskwamoziak (Pl.)	Paper Birch Trees
Maskwak (Plural)	Birch Bark
Medawihlak	Loons
Megezoak	Eagles
Mekwisagezok	Red Cedar Trees
Menonadenak	Mount Monadnock, NH
Mikoak	Squirrels
Minôbowigek peskwasawônal	Violet Flowers
Mkwazawitekw	Black River, Vermont
Môlaziganak	Black Bass
Môlôgwimenal	Wild Grapes
Môlsemok	Wolves
Mowômagw (Singular)	Fish (edible)
Mowômagok (Plural)	Fish (edible)

Moskwasak	Muskrats
Moz (Singular)	Moose
Mozak (Plural)	Moose
Msajosek	At the great hills (Massachusetts)
Mskwamagw (Sing.)	Salmon
Mskwamagok (Plural)	Salmon
Nahamak (Plural)	Turkeys
Namaskan Kisos	Fishing Moon—April
Nidôba (Singular)	Friend
Nidôbak (Plural)	Friends
Nolka (Singular)	Deer
Nolkak (Plural)	Deer
Nsôbôn	Corn Soup
Ntona	Accept
Odamôganizak	Indian Pipe
Onegígwizibó	Otter Creek, Vermont
Odzihôzo	Odzihôzo
Pabalakok	Sycamore Trees
Pezagwdamenak	Black Berries
Pezagwdamenakwamak	Black Berry Bushes
Pocumtuck	Deerfield, Massachusetts area
Sagadaboak (Plural)	Burrdock
Sagamitay	Porridge
Sasôksckak (Plural)	Sarsaparilla
Sata (Singular)	Blueberry
Satak (Plural)	Blueberries
Senikaladabagwok	Rock Tripe
Senemozi	Sugar Maple (lit. Rock Tree)
Sibosek	At the brook, a ravine at Odanak

	where the families hid during Rogers' Raid in October, 1759
Skamon (Singular)	Corn
Skamonal (Plural)	Corn
Skogadebakwol (Pl.)	Wild Ginger Roots
Sogalebi	Maple Sap
Sogalikan	Maple Sugaring
Sôgemô	Chief, Sachem (no NE term)
Sôsowipogwagak (Pl.)	Wood Sorrel
Temakwak	Beaver
Wadamobamegwezid	Brown Bear
Wadamobamegwezidak	Brown Bears
Wadebôdeb	Head (as of a family)
Wantastekw	West River, Vermont
Wantastegok	At the Wantastekw Land/Village
Wasawa (Singular)	Squash
Wasawal (Plural)	Squash
Wicinek	Eat
Wigwôm	Wigwam; house of any kind
Wijihlamid	She stays with me
Winoskík	Burlington & Colchester,VT area
Winoskitekw	Winooski River
Winos (Singular)	Onion; Wild Leek
Winosak (Plural)	Onions; Wild Leeks
Wiwniebesaki Nebes	Lake Winnipesaukee
Wizôwigid odembkwan	Yellow/Golden Haired One
Wizwame	Golden Hair
Wôbanakiak	Abenaki (in Abenaki Language)
Wôbamagwsizak (Pl.)	Shad

Wôbtegwak	Geese
Wôbimenal	Chestnuts
Wôbimizi	Chestnut Tree
Wôbimiziak	Chestnut Trees
Wôbitekw	White River, Vermont
Wôbozak (Plural)	Elk
Woronoco	Westfield, Massachusetts area
Zegweskimenak	Raspberries
Zôbapskwák	Split Rock, New York/VT on Lake Champlain

Appendix B

Native American Groups and Villages

In this book	Postcolonial (English)
Alnôbak	Human Beings/The People (original name for Abenaki)
Amiskwôlowôkoiak	Pocumtuck: People of Beaver Tail Hill; Deerfield, MA
Haudenausaunee or Hodinohso:ni	Iroquois; also known as Five Nations (pre-1760's) and Six Nations (post-1760's), and League ofhe Iroquois, & People of the Longhouse
Koasek (Place)/ Koasiak (People)	Coos, Cowasuck, Coosucks Newbury, VT & Haverhill, NH— (narrowly defined)
Kanienkehaga/ Maguak (Plural)	Mohawk; "People of the Flint" "Cowards" in Abenaki language
Mazipskoik (Place)/ Mazipskoiak (People Pl.)	Missisquoi; Swanton, VT area Missisquoi
Mohican (People)/ Mahiganek (Place)/	Mohican/Mahican People of Hudson River, New York and often used as name of the Hudson River
Muheannaheanock (Place)	The river that flows both ways Hudson River
Odanak	at the Village (in general) Also name of Odanak Abenaki village also known as St. Francis in Quebec
Sokwakiak (People)/	Sokoki/Sokwaki/Squakheag

Sokwakik (Village)	Sokoki/Sokwaki/Squakheag; Northfield, MA area)
Wôbanakiak	Abenaki/dawnland people (in Abenaki Language)
Woronoco (Village)	Westfield, MA
Woronoke (People)	Waranoke/Woronoke